KB067493

골드러시

〈K-픽션〉 시리즈는 한국문학의 젊은 상상력입니다. 최근 발표된 가장 우수하고 흥미로운 작품을 엄선하여 출간하는 〈K-픽션〉은 한국문학의 생생한 현장을 국내외 독자들과 실시간으로 공유하고자 기획되었습니다. 〈바이링궐 에디션 한국 대표 소설〉 시리즈를 통해 검증된 탁월한 번역진이 참여하여 원작의 재미와 품격을 최대한 살린 〈K-픽션〉 시리즈는 매 계절마다 새로운 작품을 선보입니다.

The K-Fiction Series represents the brightest of young imaginative voices in contemporary Korean fiction. This series spans a wide range of outstanding short stories selected by the editorial board of *ASIA* each season. These stories are then translated by professional Korean literature translators, all of whom take special care to convey the writers' original tones and nuances. We hope that these exceptional young Korean voices will delight all readers both here and abroad.

골드러시
Gold Rush

서수진 | 전미세리 옮김
Written by Seo Su-jin
Translated by Jeon Miseli

K

ASIA
PUBLISHERS

차례

Contents

골드러시
Gold Rush

진우와 서인은 끝없이 펼쳐진 붉은 흙 위를 달리고 있었다. 옆으로 에뮤 떼가 지나가기도 하고, 개를 닮은 딩고가 가만히 앉아서 둘의 차를 바라보기도 했다. 캥거루도 심심치 않게 보였는데 그때마다 진우는 긴장했다. 캥거루가 길에 뛰어들어 차에 부딪히면 차가 반파된다고 들었다. 그래서 서인이 캥거루가 바로 길옆에 있다고 외쳤을 때 진우는 곧장 브레이크를 밟으면서 차를 반대편으로 틀었다.

도로에서 아주 가까운 곳에 캥거루가 우두커니 앉아 있었다. 서인이 먼저 차에서 내리고 진우가 따라 내렸

Jin-wu was driving a car with So-in in the passenger seat along the endlessly unfolding red dirt road. At times, they saw a mob of emus passing by or a dog-like dingo sitting quietly, following the car with its eyes. Every so often, they also spotted kangaroos; and each time, Jin-wu felt quite nervous. He had been told a kangaroo might jump out into the road and crash into a car, breaking the car in half. So, no sooner had Jin-wu heard So-in yell out there was a kangaroo by the roadside than he sharply steered the wheel in the opposite direction, slamming on the brakes at the same time.

The kangaroo was sitting very close to the road,

다. 서인은 성큼성큼 도로를 건너서 캥거루에게 다가갔다. 그들이 가까이 다가가자 캥거루는 도망치려는 듯 버둥거렸으나 제대로 움직이지 못했다. 그제야 캥거루의 다리와 주변의 흙이 피로 물들어 검게 변한 것이 보였다. 캥거루는 진우와 서인을 올려다보며 머리를 힘없이 흔들었다.

"병원에 데려가야 하는 거 아니야?"

서인이 물었다.

"무슨 수로?"

"그럼 신고라도 하자."

"다친 캥거루를 구조하러 이 사막에 와달라고? 치료비는 네가 낼 거야?"

"그렇다고 그냥 둬?"

캥거루는 이제 버둥거리지도 않았다. 진우와 서인이 떠나면 딩고와 까마귀에게 산 채로 뜯어 먹히게 될 것이다. 진우는 하늘을 올려다보았다. 이글거리는 해 옆으로 검은 새 한 마리가 빙글빙글 돌고 있었다.

"예약 시간에 맞추려면 빨리 가야 해. 그만 가자."

"그냥 두고 가자고?"

"그럼 네가 남아서 뭐라도 해보든가."

looking dazed. So-in got out of the car, followed by Jin-wu. So-in strode across the road towards the kangaroo. As they got closer, the kangaroo began struggling as if wanting to get away, but in vain. Only then did they see its bloody legs and the soil around them soaked dark in blood. The kangaroo looked up at Jin-wu and So-in, its head shaking feebly.

"Shouldn't we take it to a hospital?"

So-in asked.

"But how?"

"Let's report it then, at least."

"You mean we ask them to come to this desert to rescue an injured kangaroo? And then you'll take care of the bill, huh?"

"But we can't just leave it here, can we?"

Very soon, the kangaroo stopped struggling to get up altogether. Once Jin-wu and So-in were gone, it would be torn apart and eaten up alive by the dingoes and crows. Jin-wu raised his head and looked at the sky. A black bird was circling around in the sky near the blazing sun.

"If we want to meet the reservation time, we must hurry. Let's go."

"Leave it here like this? You can't be serious."

"Well then, you can stay and do something, if you want to."

진우는 먼저 차로 돌아갔다. 서인은 그 자리에 서 있었다. 진우는 운전석에 올라 앞에 펼쳐진 길을 바라보았다. 길 끝에 물웅덩이가 있었다. 신기루였다. 진우는 눈을 감고 등받이에 머리를 기댔다. 차를 돌려서 집으로 돌아가고 싶었다.

골드러시 체험 상품이라고 했다.

지하 광산을 개조해 만든 숙소에서의 1박과 금광 체험, 오프로드를 달릴 수 있는 사륜구동 렌트카가 포함된 상품이었는데 여행사 프로모션으로 반값 할인을 한다는 거였다. 서인은 진우에게 묻지도 않고 예약한 후에 일정을 통보했다. 여행을 예약했으니 매장에 이야기해서 휴가를 내라고 했다. 진우는 요즘 식당이 바빠서 휴가를 낼 수 없다고 잘라 말했다.

"다른 사람이랑 가."

"내가 친구가 어딨어."

서인과 나누는 대화는 늘 이런 식이었다. 서인은 자신의 상황을 자학적으로 깔아뭉갰고, 그렇게 된 데에 진우의 책임이 있다고 추궁하는 것처럼 들렸다.

"그럼 혼자 다녀오든가."

Jin-wu returned to the car. But So-in just stood there, refusing to leave the spot. Sitting in the driver's seat, Jin-wu gazed at the road ahead stretching into the distance. Far away where the road faded, he saw a pool of water. A mirage. He closed his eyes and leaned back, resting his head on the back of the seat. He wanted to turn the car around and go back home.

It was a travel package called "Experience the Gold Rush."

Included in the package were a one-night stay at an underground lodge that had been converted from a mine, a firsthand experience of gold mine, and a car rental, that is, a four-wheel drive vehicle, all at a half price as part of the travel agency's promotion programs. So-in, without even checking with Jin-wu, made a reservation and later simply announced their travel plan to Jin-wu. She also suggested that he should talk to the manager and get a couple days off since she had already made a reservation. Jin-wu flatly refused to do so, saying that the restaurant was too busy at the time for him to take a vacation.

"Why don't you go with someone else?"

"You know that I've got no friends."

Conversation with So-in was always like that. She

"렌트카를 빌려주는 거라니까."

서인은 운전을 하지 못했다. 그러니까 이 대화는 서인이 혼자 장을 보러 가지도 못하고, 어디를 외출하고 싶어도 진우의 도움을 빌려야 하는 처지인데 진우는 늘 바쁘다는 것으로 향해 가는 게 분명했다.

"그럼 취소해."

"프로모션 상품이라 취소 못해."

"내가 위약금 낼게."

서인은 말없이 진우를 쏘아보았다. 쌍꺼풀이 짙고 커다란 눈은 한때 진우가 수없이 입을 맞췄던 것이었다. 그녀의 작고 낮은 코와 얇은 입술도 못 견디게 사랑했었다. 그러나 이제는 그 모든 것들이 서인의 유약하고 의존적인 성격을 드러내는 것만 같았다.

"결혼 7주년이야."

둘은 첫 번째 결혼기념일 이후로 한 번도 결혼기념일을 챙긴 적이 없었다. 그런데 이제 와 결혼기념일이라니. 진우는 후에 곱씹을수록 화가 났지만 서인이 처음 말을 꺼냈을 때는 7년이라는 시간에 압도되어서 다른 말을 하지 못했다. 서인과 7년을 부부로 지내왔다니 믿을 수 없었다. 언제 시간이 그렇게 흘렀던가. 무슨 생각

would self-disparagingly put down the situations she was in, somehow making it sound like an accusation that Jin-wu was responsible for her sorry state of affairs.

"Why don't you go alone, then?"

"What about the car rental?"

So-in couldn't drive. Obviously, So-in was, as usual, leading the conversation to an insinuation: Jin-wu knew full well she was unable to go grocery shopping or on an outing without his help, and yet he was always busy.

"Cancel it, then."

"It's a promotion package, I can't cancel it."

"I'll pay the penalty."

So-in silently glared at Jin-wu. There had been times when Jin-wu countlessly kissed those big, beautiful, double-lid eyes. He used to be hopelessly in love with her small, flat nose and thin lips, too. But now, all of them seemed only to reveal So-in's weak and dependent personality.

"It's our seventh wedding anniversary, for God's sake."

The two had never celebrated their wedding anniversaries except the first one. Why then celebrate it now after all these years? The more he thought about it, the more furious he got. But when So-in brought up the subject, he couldn't say anything at

으로 7년이라는 시간을 보내온 건지 알 수 없었다.

진우와 서인은 7년 전에 한국에서 혼인신고를 했고, 그로부터 3개월 전에 퍼스의 셰어하우스에서 처음 만났다.

퍼스는 호주 서쪽의 도시로 시드니나 멜버른에 비해 인구가 적었고 그래서 일자리를 찾기가 더 쉬웠다. 당시 진우가 일하는 일식당은 퍼스의 시내에 있었는데 식당에서 가까운 곳에 아파트를 렌트해 직원들의 셰어하우스로 사용했다. 방 세 칸짜리 아파트에 직원 열 명이 살았고, 진우와 서인은 거실을 나눠 썼다.

거실 한가운데 커튼을 치고 서인은 소파에서, 진우는 바닥에 얇은 폼매트리스를 깔아놓고 잤다. 주방에서 일하는 진우의 출근 시간이 홀에서 일하는 서인보다 일렀기 때문에 진우의 알람이 먼저 울렸다. 진우가 아무리 서둘러 알람을 끄고 조심스럽게 이불을 개도 서인은 이내 일어났다.

"지금 나가는 거야?"

커튼 뒤에서 서인은 잠이 묻은 목소리로 물었다. 진우는 깨워서 미안하다고 말하고는 얼른 옷가지를 챙겨

first, overwhelmed by the sheer number of years of their marriage. Seven years! It was hard to believe he and So-in had been a husband and wife for as long as seven years. Time had sped by unawares to him. What on earth had he been thinking while spending those seven long years? He had no idea.

Jin-wu and So-in registered their marriage in Korea three months after they met for the first time at a share house in Perth.

Perth, a city in the western part of Australia, was less densely populated than Sydney or Melbourne, so it was easier for Jin-wu to find a job there. The Japanese restaurant where Jin-wu worked at the time was located downtown and its employees rented a flat near the restaurant and used it as their share house. The ten of them lived in that three-bedroom flat; and Jin-wu and So-in shared the living room.

A curtain divided the living room, and So-in slept on the couch on one side; on the other, Jin-wu slept on a thin foam mattress spread on the floor. Jin-wu who worked in the kitchen had to get to the restaurant earlier than So-in, one of the hall staff. Whenever Jin-wu's alarm went off first, he would quickly turn it off and put away his bedding as quietly as possible; nevertheless, So-in would immedi-

서 일어났다. 세수하는 내내 서인이 다시 잠들지 못하는 건 아닐까 걱정했다. 그러나 서인은 그것에 대해 불평하는 법이 없었다. 오히려 셰어생들이 다 같이 술을 마실 때면 꼭 진우 옆에 앉아서 전날 자신이 코를 골지는 않았냐며 살갑게 말을 걸었다. 둘이 사귀게 된 날 밤에는 술에 취해 진우의 어깨에 머리를 기대고 진우와 거실을 나눠 써서 다행이라고 했다. 자신은 잠드는 것이 어려운데 진우가 잠든 후에 내는 고른 숨소리가 백색소음처럼 심리적인 안정을 준다는 거였다.

연애를 시작하면서 둘은 바로 비자에 대해 논의하기 시작했다. 서인의 워킹홀리데이 비자가 끝나가고 있었다. 서인은 비자가 만료되면 한국으로 돌아가고 싶어 했다. 그러나 진우는 이미 식당 사장으로부터 457 비자 지원을 약속받은 후였다.

457 비자를 약속받기까지 진우는 최저시급의 70퍼센트만 받으며 일했다. 휴식 시간에도 쉬지 않았고 시프트로 받은 시간보다 매일 서너 시간씩 더 일했다. 사장은 진우의 휴무일에도 때때로 그를 불러서 종일 매장 재고 정리를 시키고 밥을 한 끼 사주고 들여보내고는 했다. 457 비자 신청 이후에는 최저시급으로 계산

ately wake up.

"Are you leaving now?"

Jin-wu would hear So-in's half-asleep, muffled voice coming from behind the curtain. He then would say he was sorry to have waken her up, and quickly gather up his clothes and leave the room. While washing his face, he kept worrying that So-in might not be able to go back to sleep. However, So-in never complained about it. On the contrary, whenever the share house residents got together to have a drink, she never failed to sit right beside Jin-wu and started a friendly conversation, asking him if she hadn't snored the night before. On the night they began dating, she got drunk and leaned her head on Jin-wu's shoulder and said she was lucky to share the living room with him. She had trouble falling asleep before, but now Jin-wu's regular breathing in sleep calmed her down like the psychological effects of white noise.

Not long after they began dating, the two got right down to discussing the issues of their visa status. So-in's working holiday visa would expire soon. Once her visa expired, she said, she wanted to go back to Korea. As for Jin-wu, however, the restaurant owner had already promised to support his 457 visa application.

Until he was promised the 457 visa application,

한 연봉보다 훨씬 웃도는 법정 금액을 지급해야 했기 때문에, 진우는 통장에 들어오는 급여의 절반을 사장에게 현금으로 되돌려주기로 약속했다. 사업체가 지급해야 하는 비자 신청비나 변호사비 따위도 모두 진우가 내기로 했다.

따지고 보면 불법이 아닌 것이 없었지만 그건 호주 업체에 해당하는 이야기였고 한인 업체에서는 관례로 여겨지는 일들이었다. 진우뿐만이 아니라 한인 식당, 한인 슈퍼, 한인 여행사에서 일하는 한국인들은 모두 그런 대우를 받으며 일했다. 457 비자를 신청해준다는 명목으로 주에 50시간씩 일을 시키면서 주급으로 100불만을 주는 업체도 있었다. 2년을 무상으로 일해주고 비자를 얻는 것과 마찬가지였다. 그러니 진우의 사장은 악덕 업주 축에도 끼지 못한다고들 했다. 진우 역시 부당한 처우에 불평하기보다는 자신이 비자를 받을 수 있다는 사실을 기쁘게 생각했다.

457 비자로 2년을 일하면 영주권을 신청할 수 있었다. 그러면 많은 것이 달라질 거였다. 급여는 적어도 두 배, 경력을 고려하면 세 배가 될 터였고 법정 유급휴가 4주에 공공의료와 공교육이 무료였다. 진우는 한국에

Jin-wu had to settle for taking only 70 percent of the minimum wage. He never took breaks and everyday worked three or four hours longer than the number of hours assigned to his shift. Often, the owner asked Jin-wu to come into work even on his days off and had him take an inventory of the sales floor the whole day. The owner then treated Jin-wu to a meal before letting him go back to the share house. Once Jin-wu's application for the 457 visa was filed, the law obliged the restaurant owner to raise Jin-wu's annual salary to a much higher level than the pervious one which had been calculated at the rate of minimum wage. The situation forced Jin-wu to promise to return to the owner a half of the pay that would be deposited in his bank account, of course, in cash. Jin-wu also had to agree to take care of the visa application fee, the lawyer's fee, and so on, which the business owner was supposed to pay.

To speak the truth, there were no dealings that were not illegal; nonetheless, debating the legality was applicable only to the Australian businesses. As far as the Korean businesses were concerned, such dealings were accepted and smoothed over as conventions. Not only Jin-wu but also all the other Koreans working in the Korean restaurants, Korean supermarkets, or Korean travel agencies were

서는 누릴 수 없는 것들을 약속하며 서인을 설득했다.

한국에서 혼인신고를 하고 돌아온 이후에도 비자 문제가 남아 있었다. 457 비자를 신청하기 위해서는 영어 점수가 필요했는데 주에 72시간씩 일하는 진우로서는 공부할 시간을 내기가 쉽지 않았다. 필요한 점수를 받으려면 일을 그만두고 몇 달간 시험 준비에 전념해야 했다. 진우의 시급이 서인보다 높았고 홀에서 영어로 서빙을 하는 서인의 영어 실력이 진우에 비해 훨씬 나았으므로, 진우가 일을 하고 서인은 영어 공부를 하기로 했다. 그렇게 진우 대신 서인의 이름으로 비자 신청을 하게 되었다.

그 후로는 모든 일이 순조롭게 흘러갔다. 서인은 영어 시험에서 좋은 점수를 받았고, 오래지 않아 서인의 이름으로 457 비자가 나왔다. 진우는 곧장 파트너 비자를 신청했다. 진우의 파트너 비자까지 승인이 난 후에 진우와 서인은 마스터룸으로 이사하기로 했다.

진우가 한국 교민 웹사이트에서 괜찮은 셰어하우스를 찾았다. 한국인 마스터가 렌트한 아파트를 한국인 셰어생들에게 다시 렌트하는 식이었다. 진우와 서인은 보증금과 함께 한 달 치 렌트비를 완납하고 마스터룸

treated in the same way. In the name of supporting the employee's 457 visa application, some business owners paid their workers only 100 dollars for the 50-hour workweek. It meant working without pay for two years in order to get the visa. Compared to those business owners, some people said, Jin-wu's employer didn't even deserve to be called an evil business owner. Jin-wu himself, rather than complaining about his employer's unfairness, considered himself lucky to be able to get the visa at all.

Once his 457 visa was approved, two more years of work would qualify Jin-wu to apply for the permanent residentship. The new status would bring so many changes into his life, for example, the pay rise, doubled at the least or even tripled when his seniority was taken into account, four-week statutory paid vacation, and free public health care and public education. Promising all the benefits they could never afford to enjoy in Korea, Jin-wu finally won So-in over.

When they came back to Perth after registering their marriage, they still had the visa problems to deal with. They needed a passing grade in the English proficiency test in order to apply for the 457 visa. For Jin-wu who had to work 72 hours a week, making time to practice English was not easy. To get the required level of proficiency, he needed

을 얻었다. 마스터룸에는 욕조가 딸린 화장실이 있었다. 둘은 그날 밤 오랜 시간 목욕을 했다.

　이사하고 사흘이 지난 저녁, 경찰이 찾아왔고 당장 집을 비우라고 했다. 렌트비와 공과금을 3개월 연체했다는 것이 이유였다. 경찰은 한 시간을 줄 테니 필요한 물건을 챙기라고 했고 진우와 서인은 책상과 옷장, 서랍장 사이를 뛰어다니며 노트북과 옷가지, 신발을 각자의 캐리어에 마구잡이로 구겨 넣었다. 가구와 가전은 모두 마스터의 것이었으나 폐기 처분된다는 경찰의 말에 진우는 서인에게 캐리어를 맡기고 텔레비전을 들었다. 한국인 마스터는 전화를 받지 않았다. 진우는 주변의 한인들을 수소문해, 마스터가 수명의 셰어생들에게서 보증금과 월세를 챙겨 한국으로 돌아갔다는 것을 알게 되었다.

　그 후 식당의 셰어하우스로 돌아가 한 달간 거실에서 지내면서 서인은 호주 부동산에 직접 찾아가 집을 구했다. 부동산 업자가 날짜를 정해 집을 공개하는 인스펙션에 참가해 아파트를 꼼꼼히 살폈다. 세 번의 인스펙션에 다녀온 후에 서인은 한 곳을 골라 렌트 신청서를 작성했다.

to quit his job and concentrate on preparing for the test for at least several months. Jin-wu's hourly wage was more than So-in's; and So-in who was a hall server spoke English much better than Jin-wu did. Therefore, Jin-wu agreed to continue working and So-in to study English for the test. That was why So-in, not Jin-wu, ended up applying for the 457 visa.

From then on, everything went smoothly. So-in got a good grade in the language test and before long, she was granted the 457 visa. Jin-wu immediately applied for a partner visa. After the partner visa was also approved, Jin-wu and So-in decided to move to a Master Room.

Jin-wu found a decent share flat in the website operated for the Korean residents. One Korean Master rented a flat, which was in turn rented out to Korean flat sharers. Jin-wu and So-in paid in full the first month rent and the deposit and moved into the master bedroom of the flat, which had an *en suite* bathroom with a bathtub in it. On that first night, the couple took their own sweet time bathing.

Three days after their move, the police showed up in the evening and asked them to vacate the apartment right away because the rents and public utilities payments had been overdue for three

"중요한 건 중국인들과 싸워 이기는 거야."

서인은 비장하게 말했다.

"중국사람들은 아파트가 마음에 들면 제시된 렌트비에서 30불을 올려서 신청서를 낸대."

서인은 35불을 올려서 냈다. 사장에게 추천서를 받아 진우의 급여명세서와 함께 제출했다. 은행 잔고 증명을 위해 입출금 내역서도 제출해야 했는데, 서인은 주변에서 돈을 빌려 진우의 통장 잔고를 불려놨다. 그렇게 렌트 승인을 받았다.

이사하던 날 진우와 서인은 그들만의 아파트에서 창문을 활짝 열어놓고 삼겹살을 구웠고, 소주를 다섯 병이나 비웠다. 둘은 얼굴이 붉게 달아오른 채로 그들 앞에 펼쳐진 미래에 대해 이야기했다. 아이가 마음껏 뛰어놀 수 있도록 정원이 딸린 집을 살 것이다. 크리스마스 휴가에 바닷가의 집을 한 달간 빌릴 것이다. 아이의 방학이면 캠핑카를 타고 호주의 사막을 여행하며 반짝이는 별로 가득 찬 밤하늘을 하염없이 바라볼 것이다. 서인은 마치 그 모든 것들을 바라보고 있기라도 한 듯이 환하게 빛나는 얼굴을 했다. 진우는 서인의 말에 그래, 그래, 대답하면서 고개를 끄덕였다.

months. The policemen gave them one hour to pack up their things. Jin-wu and So-in rushed around from the desk to the wardrobe to the chest of drawers, cramming their laptops, clothes, and shoes into their respective wheeled suitcases. All the furniture and electric appliances belonged to the Master, but when the police said everything that was left behind would be discarded, Jin-wu, handing So-in his suitcase, picked up the TV. The Korean Master didn't answer the phone. So, Jin-wu asked around and learned from some Koreans around him that the Master had pocketed the deposits and rents from a number of flat sharers, and returned to Korea.

After the incident, Jin-wu and So-in went back to the same place shared with the other restaurant workers and stayed there in the living room for a month, during which time So-in visited Australian real-estate agencies in person to inquire about a place for rent. She went to the open-house events scheduled by the realtors and meticulously inspected each flat. After the third such inspection, So-in made a choice and filled out the rent application form.

"Winning the battle against the Chinese, that's the key to success."

So-in said resolutely.

"정말 좋겠지."

서인의 말에 진우는 대답 대신 손을 뻗어 서인의 얼굴을 쓰다듬었다.

그날 밤 그 누구도 누워본 적이 없는 새 침대에 누워서 진우는 자신이 서인을 얼마나 사랑하는지 말하고 싶었으나 서인은 이미 잠들어 있었다. 서인은 이제 진우보다 먼저 잠들 때가 많았고, 아침에 진우가 나갈 때도 잠에서 깨지 않았다. 진우는 서인의 잠든 얼굴을 바라보면서 서인을 만나다니 정말 운이 좋다, 더 열심히 살아야지, 그런 생각을 했다. 그리고 1년 후 서인이 다른 남자와 잤다는 걸 알게 되었다.

홀에 새로 들어온 스물두 살 남자애였다. 전체 회식을 하면서 진우와 몇 마디를 나누기도 했었다. 아직 여드름 자국이 남아 있고 말끝마다 욕설을 내뱉는 애였다. 서인은 그 남자애를 사랑한다고 했다. 그 남자애도 서인을 사랑한다고 했다면서 같이 한국으로 돌아가겠다고 했다. 진우에게 미안하다며 울었지만 정작 진우가 화를 내자 서인은 더 크게 소리쳤다.

"내가 얼마나 외로웠는지 알기는 해? 여기에는 가족도 친구도 없는데 너는 늘 바쁘고."

"The Chinese applicants, if they like a flat, offer to pay extra 30 dollars on top of the original rent."

So-in said and offered a 35-dollar top-up herself when she submitted the application form, along with a reference letter from the restaurant owner and a copy of Jin-wu's pay stub. Their bank statement was also part of the required documents to prove they had sufficient funds. So-in borrowed money from the people she knew to raise Jin-wu's account balance. Her efforts paid off in the end, and the rent was approved.

On the day they moved into the flat that was shared with no one else but each other, Jin-wu and So-in kept the windows wide open while grilling pork belly and drinking five bottles of *soju*. With their faces flushed red, they talked about their future they envisioned. They would buy a house with a garden so that their children could play there to their heart's content. On Christmas holidays, they would rent a cottage by the sea for a month. When the children were on vacation, they would travel through the Australian deserts in a camping car, gazing up for the longest time at the night skies filled with twinkling stars. As if she was really gazing at them there and then, So-in's face shone brightly. Jin-wu kept nodding his head, saying "Yes, yes, yes."

진우는 서인을 때리고 싶었다. 뺨을 갈기고 그 작은 어깨를 잡아 마구 흔들고 싶었다. 둘 다 죽여버리겠다고 소리치고 싶었다. 그러나 그럴 수 없었다. 몇 주에 걸쳐서 같은 싸움을 계속하는 동안 진우에게 점점 더 명확하게 다가온 것은 서인이 돌아간다면 진우의 비자가 취소되어버린다는 거였다.

헤드셰프로 일하면서 457 비자를 얻어낸 것은 진우였지만 서류상에는 서인의 이름으로 되어 있었다. 진우는 서인의 파트너 자격으로 거주를 허락받은 것뿐이었다. 진우가 영어 점수를 받고 다시 비자를 신청하기까지 시간이 얼마나 걸릴지 알 수 없었다. 한번 비자가 취소되면 그 후로는 다시 받기가 더 어려워진다는 것도 잘 알고 있었다.

진우는 서인에게 한국에 가지 말라고 했다. 처음에는 비자를 이유로 들지 않았지만 결국 영주권을 받을 때까지만 기다려달라고 했다. 서인은 그렇게는 살 수 없다고 했다.

"나 걔랑 잤어. 내가 너랑 어떻게 살아."

"네가 정 원하면 걔랑 가서 살아."

진우는 서인에게 무릎을 꿇었다.

"It'll be really wonderful, won't it?"

Instead of chiming in, Jin-wu reached out his hand to stroke her face.

That night, lying in the new bed that no one had ever slept in, Jin-wu wanted to tell So-in how much he loved her. But So-in was already asleep. From then on, So-in quite often fell asleep before Jin-wu did and didn't even wake up in the morning when he left home for work. But still, Jin-wu would look at her sleeping face and tell himself, "I'm so lucky to have met So-in. I'll try harder to have an earnest life with her." A year later, however, he came to learn that So-in had slept with another man.

It was a young man, twenty-two years old, who had just joined the hall staff. He and Jin-wu even had a brief chat together at a staff dinner. He still had acne scars on his face and had a tendency to end his utterances with swearwords. So-in said she was in love with the young man who had told her that he loved her too. So-in wanted to go back to Korea with him. She cried while apologizing to Jin-wu, but when he got angry, she shouted louder than he did.

"D'you even know how lonely I've been? I've got no family, no friends here, and yet you're always busy."

Jin-wu wanted to beat her, slap her in the face,

"제발 1년만 기다려줘. 그냥 호주에만 있어줘, 제발. 부탁이야."

숙소에 도착했을 때는 벌써 해가 저물어가고 있었다. 버려진 경주의 고분처럼 보이는 낮은 언덕에 문이 나 있었다. 문을 여니 어두컴컴한 계단이 아래로 향해 있었다. 양쪽 벽에 달린 작은 램프에서 희미한 빛이 새어 나왔지만 그래도 발아래 바닥이 선명하게 보이지 않았다.

리셉션에는 아무도 없었다. 한참을 기다려도 아무도 나오지 않았다. 서인이 이메일을 뒤져 전화를 걸어보았지만 상대가 전화를 받지 않는 듯했다. 진우는 서인이 잘못 예약한 거라고 생각했다. 프로모션은 처음부터 사기였던 것이다. 골드러시 같은 허황한 이름에 속아 넘어간 서인 탓이다.

진우는 서인을 몰아세우고 싶었다. 이게 도대체 뭐냐고, 오지 말자고 하지 않았냐고, 결혼기념일 여행이라니 처음부터 말도 안 되는 거였다고. 그때 복도 끝에서 한 남자가 걸어 나왔다.

배가 한껏 나온 백인 남자가 만면에 웃음을 띠고 인

grab her by her small shoulders and shake her as hard as he could. He felt compelled to yell at her that he would kill both of them. But he couldn't do that. Over the following several weeks, they had the same quarrel over and over. But then, it gradually occurred to Jin-wu that if So-in went back to Korea, his partner visa would be cancelled.

Although credit must have gone to Jin-wu who had worked hard as a head chef in order to obtain the 457 visa, it was So-in's name that was written on the visa in the end. Jin-wu was allowed to reside in the country only in the capacity of a partner to So-in. He didn't know how long it would take for him to get the required English test results before he became qualified to apply for the visa again. He was well aware that once the visa was cancelled, it would be harder to get it issued the second time.

Jin-wu asked So-in not to go back to Korea. At first, he didn't bring up the subject of visa. In the end, however, he asked her to wait only until his permanent residentship was approved. So-in insisted that she couldn't live like that.

"I've slept with him. How on earth can I keep on living with you?"

"If you really want to go live with him now, I won't stop you."

Jin-wu kneeled down before So-in.

사를 했다. 남자는 양팔을 벌리면서 자신이 주인이라
고 했다.

"시원하지 않냐고. 여긴 냉방이 필요가 없대."

서인이 주인의 말을 옮겨 주었다. 반팔을 입은 진우
의 팔에 닭살이 돋았다. 서인을 흘긋 돌아보니 양팔을
끌어안고 있었다.

주인은 진우와 서인을 이끌고 숙소의 이곳저곳을 보
여주었다. 서인은 하나하나 진우에게 통역해주었다.

"저녁은 여기에서 먹는 거래. 계산은 체크아웃할 때
하면 된다고 하네. 여기서는 별이 잘 보이니까 꼭 봐야
한대. 별을 보려면 이쪽으로 나가면 된다네. 이 복도 끝
에 유리문이 있는데 잠겨 있으니 들어올 때 꼭 다시 잠
가달래. 곧장 외부로 통하는 문이라 문단속을 잘해야
한다고."

좁은 복도의 벽과 천장이 둥그렇게 이어져 있었다.
울퉁불퉁한 표면이 하나의 거대한 암석의 단면으로 보
였다. 주인은 진우와 서인의 방에 먼저 들어가 불을 켜
주었다. 낮은 조도의 조명 아래 흡사 동굴 같은 방이 드
러났다. 허리까지 올라오는 높은 침대가 중앙에 놓여
있었고, 양옆으로 협탁과 옷장이 자리하고 있었다. 옷

"But please, wait just one year. Just stay a year in Australia, please. I'm begging you."

When they arrived at the lodge, it was getting dark already. At the foot of a low hill that looked like an abandoned ancient tomb in Kyongju was a door. Opening the door, they saw in the dim light a flight of stairs leading downwards. Faint light escaped from the small lamps installed on both sides of the wall, but still they were unable to see cleary the floor under their feet.

There was no one at the reception. They waited quite a while, but still no one showed up. So-in found the phone number in the email and called the lodge, but there seemed to be no answer. Jin-wu thought So-in must have got something wrong. Perhaps, the promotion package was a fraud from the beginning. She had been fooled by the vain name like "Gold Rush."

Jin-wu felt an urge to berate So-in, backing her into a corner. What the hell is this? Didn't I tell you we shouldn't come here? Wedding anniversary, huh? It didn't make any sense at all from the first. Just then, he saw a man at the far end of the hallway walking out towards them.

The caucasian man with a big potbelly and a big smile all over his face greeted them. Opening

장 옆에는 작은 화장실로 통하는 문이 있었다. 침대의 헤드와 옷장, 그리고 협탁과 화장실 문까지 모두 짙은 밤색에 별다른 장식이 없는 네모난 모양이었다. 골드러시 체험 상품의 숙소라기에는 지나치게 검소하고 음울해 보였다.

주인이 나가고 서인은 울퉁불퉁한 벽을 만져보면서 방의 여기저기를 둘러보았다. 진우는 침대 위에 털썩 누웠다. 매트리스는 딱딱했고 벽돌색과 겨자색이 섞인 체크무늬 이불은 축축한 냉기를 품고 있었다. 진우는 오래 운전을 해서인지 몹시 피곤했다. 저절로 눈이 감겼다. 그때 서인이 비명을 질렀다. 진우는 반사적으로 몸을 일으켰다. 서인이 화장실 문에서 튀어나왔고, 진우는 화장실로 뛰어들어갔다. 변기 안쪽에 누런 개구리가 붙어 있었다. 한 뼘이 족히 될 법했다.

"어떻게 해?"

서인이 소리쳤다. 진우는 물을 내렸다. 개구리가 물길을 거슬러 펄쩍 뛰어올랐다. 서인이 다시 비명을 질렀다. 진우는 개구리의 뒤를 따라다니며 발을 쿵쿵 굴러 복도로 내몰았다. 개구리가 복도의 어둠 속으로 사라지는 것을 확인한 후에 진우는 방으로 돌아왔다. 서

his arms, the man introduced himself as the lodge owner.

"Isn't it nice and cool down here? he says. No air conditioning is necessary in this lodge, he says."

So-in interpreted for Jin-wu what the owner had said. Jin-wu in a short-sleave shirt felt goose bumps on his arms. He glanced at So-in; she had her arms folded.

The owner showed Jin-wu and So-in here and there around the lodge. So-in repeated to Jin-wu all of the owner's remarks in Korean, word by word.

"We'll eat dinner here. We can take care of the bill when we check out. This is a perfect place for star-gazing, a must do for visitors, he says. If we want to see the stars, this is the way we take to go outside. At the end of this hallway, there is a glass door that is locked. So, when we come back in, we need to make sure to lock the door again. It opens directly onto the outside, so must stay securely locked at all times.

The walls and the ceiling of the narrow hallway together formed an arch. The uneven surface of the arch looked like the cross section of a gigantic rock. The owner entered their reserved room ahead of them to turn on the lights. The low-voltage lights revealed a cave-like room. In the center of the room was a bed the top of which came up to his

인이 눈을 크게 뜨고 진우의 얼굴을 살폈다.

"갔어."

서인이 그제야 한숨을 쉬면서 침대에 털썩 앉았다.

"고마워."

진우는 대답하지 않았다.

숙소의 식당에는 진우와 서인뿐이었다. 둘이 테이블에 자리를 잡자 주인이 다가와 메뉴를 설명했다.

"지금은 스테이크만 가능하대. 사이드로 감자튀김이 나오고. 어떻게 할래?"

진우는 나도 그 정도는 알아듣는다고 말하려다 말았다.

"뭘 물어보는 거야? 그냥 된다는 거 시켜."

"와인도 한 잔 시킬게."

"그러든지."

주인은 와인 잔과 와인병을 들고 와서는 그대로 두고 갔다.

"얼마 안 남았다고 다 먹으래. 꽤 남은 거 같은데 인심이 좋네, 여기."

와인 뚜껑을 열자 알코올 냄새가 강하게 올라왔다.

waist. A side table was on one side of the bed and a wardrobe on the other. Beside the wardrobe, there was a door to a small bathroom. The headboard of the bed, the wardrobe, the side table, and even the door to the bathroom were all dark brown in color and rectangular in shape, and had no particular designs or embellishment. For a lodge as part of the "Experience the Gold Rush" travel package, it seemed much too frugal and gloomy.

After the lodge owner left the room, So-in began to take a good look around the room, touching the uneven walls here and there. Jin-wu flopped down and stretched out on the bed. The mattress was hard; and the plaided, burgundy and mustard-colored comforter was damp and cold to the touch. Jin-wu felt very tired; perhaps because it had been too long a drive. He couldn't keep his eyes open. As soon as he closed his eyes, he heard So-in's scream. In a reflex action, he sat bolt upright. As So-in burst out of the bathroom, Jin-wu ran into it. Sticking to the inner surface of the toilet bowl was a yellowish frog, a hand span long.

"What should we do?"

So-in hollered. Jin-wu flushed the toilet. The frog instantly jumped up against the flushing water. So-in screamed again. Jin-wu kept chasing the frog, stamping his foot, out of the room and into the

오래전에 따놓은 모양이었다. 주인이 내온 스테이크는 너무 바짝 익혀서 질겼고, 감자튀김은 포크로 찍으면 으스러져서 손으로 집어 먹어야 했다. 그러나 서인은 맛있다고 했다. 진우가 대답하지 않자 이렇게 외진 곳에서 이 정도면 감지덕지라는 말을 덧붙였다. 식사를 다 마친 후에 서인은 별을 보자고 했다.

주인이 알려준 대로 복도를 따라가서 유리문을 열고 나가니 언덕의 봉우리였다. 하늘에는 많은 별이 떠 있었다. 어찌나 많은지 별처럼 보이지 않고 창문에 잔뜩 낀 먼지처럼 보였다. 바람이 매섭게 불었다. 서인은 춥다며 먼저 들어갔다. 진우도 따라 들어가려 했는데 서인의 뒤로 문이 닫혔다. 진우가 문을 열려고 할 때 서인이 안쪽에서 문고리를 잡고 있는 것이 보였다.

"뭐 하는 거야? 문 열어."

바람 소리가 귀에 울려서 안에서 서인이 입을 벙긋거리는 건 보였지만 말소리는 들리지 않았다. 어쩌면 입만 벙긋거리고 있는 건지도 몰랐다. 문을 흔들었는데 열리지 않았다. 서인이 여전히 안에서 문을 붙잡고 있었다. 깜깜한 밤이었고, 바람이 심하게 부는 언덕 위였다. 진우는 거칠게 문을 흔들었다.

hallway. After making sure that the reptile had disappeared into the darkness of the hallway, Jin-wu came back to the room. With her eyes wide open, So-in studied Jin-wu's face.

"It's gone."

So-in finally sighed with relief and flopped herself down on the bed.

"Thank you."

Jin-wu didn't respond.

Jin-wu and So-in were the only guests in the dining room. When they sat at a table, the owner came to them and explained the day's menu.

"He says they can only prepare the steak dish this evening. With chips on the side. What d'ya think?"

Jin-wu was about to say, "I'm capable of understanding at least that much, too." But he checked himself.

"What on earth is there to think about? Just order whatever they can serve now."

"I'll order a glass of wine as well."

"As you wish."

The owner brought two glasses and a bottle of wine. He then left their table, leaving the wine bottle still on the table.

"He says there isn't much left in the bottle anyway, so we may drink it up. By the look of it, there's

"씨발, 장난치지 마."

순간 문이 벌컥 열렸고, 문고리를 잡고 있던 서인이 중심을 잃고 진우 쪽으로 쓰러졌다.

"왜 이딴 장난을 치고 그래?"

"나는 문을 열려고 한 거야. 안에서 문이 잠겨버렸다고."

서인은 울먹거렸다. 진우는 서인을 밀치고 복도로 들어섰다. 진우의 등으로 바람이 몰아쳤다.

그 일이 있고 진우는 한밤에 서인이 흐느끼는 소리에 잠을 깰 때가 있었다. 그럴 때면 참을 수 없이 화가 났다. 서인을 발로 걷어차고 한국으로 돌아가라고 소리치고 싶었다. 그러나 그러지 않았다. 처음에는 영주권 때문이라고 생각했다. 하지만 영주권을 받은 이후에도 진우는 서인에게 이제 돌아가도 좋다고 말하지 않았다. 말하지 않아도 서인이 떠날 거라고 여겼다. 서인이 "이젠 됐지."라고 말하며 캐리어를 들고 집을 나서는 꿈을 꾸기도 했다. 그러나 서인은 떠나지 않았다. 대신 진우의 이름으로 장기주택자금 대출을 받자고 했다. 서인은 아파트를 구했던 때처럼 혼자 은행과 부동

still quite a bit left. It's a generous place, here."

When Jin-wu uncorked the bottle, a strong smell of alcohol assailed his nostrils. Probably, the bottle had long been opened. The steak brought out by the owner was much too well done and chewy; the chips got squished when in contact with the fork, so they had to use their fingers to eat them. But So-in said the food was delicious. When she didn't get Jin-wu's response, she added that considering how isolated the place was, the food quality there deserved at least that much appreciation. After dinner, So-in proposed to go watch the stars.

As the owner had told them, they walked through the hallway, unlocked the glass door, and stepped outside. The peak of the hill rushed into sight. The sky was densely dotted with stars, so many that they didn't even look like stars; instead, they appeared to be dust caked thick on a window. The place was being whipped by the wind. Soon, So-in went back inside alone, saying that it was too cold out there. Jin-wu was about to enter the building himself, following So-in, but the door suddenly shut behind her. Jin-wu was trying to open the door when he saw So-in clutching the door handle inside the door.

"What're you doing? Open the door."

He saw So-in telling him something, but he

산을 바쁘게 다닌 후에 외곽의 단독주택을 찾았다. 북향이라 해가 잘 들고 뒤뜰이 넓은 집이었다. 서인은 뒤뜰에 색색의 꽃과 딸기, 토마토 모종을 심었다. 진우는 휴일 오후에 주방 식탁에 앉아 뒤뜰에 앉은 서인의 뒷모습을 지켜볼 때가 많았다. 서인은 챙이 넓은 밀짚모자를 쓰고 손을 재바르게 움직여 흙을 뒤집고 씨를 심고 잡초를 뽑고 잎을 솎아냈다. 하루가 다르게 뒤뜰이 풍성해졌다. 가지와 호박이 열렸고, 서인이 세워놓은 대를 타고 줄기콩과 토마토가 자랐다. 서인은 종종 뒤뜰에서 딴 채소들로 샐러드를 만들었지만 진우는 손도 대지 않았다. 서인은 국이나 반찬을 남기는 한이 있어도 샐러드는 다 먹었다. 한 번씩 상자에 담아 진우의 차 트렁크에 싣고는 매장에서 쓰라고도 했다. 그러면 진우는 매장 가는 길에 공원에 들러 쓰레기통에 상자째로 버렸다. 언젠가부터 서인은 뒤뜰 가꾸는 것을 그만두었고, 이제 뒤뜰에는 이름을 알 수 없는 풀이 허리까지 올라와 있었다. 진우는 버려진 정글처럼 보이는 뒤뜰을 바라보면서 어느 편이 더 나은지 알 수 없었다. 먹지도 않는 채소들이 가득한 뜰과 보기 흉한 잡초로 뒤덮인 뜰 중에 무엇이 더 나쁜지 도무지 알 수가 없었다.

couldn't hear her because of the deafening roar of the wind. Suddenly a suspicion crossed his mind: she may be pretending to say something; in fact, she is not saying anything but simply opening and closing her mouth. He shook the door, to no avail. So-in was still holding onto the door handle inside. It was dark out there with no lights; worse still, he was on top of a hill that was being thrashed by bitter winds. He shook the door again, violently.

"What the fuck, stop this bullshit right now."

At that moment, the door burst open and So-in, with her hands still on the door handle, lost her balance and fell towards Jin-wu.

"What's the matter with you, pulling a prank like that?"

"I was just trying to open the door for you. Somehow it had got locked from inside."

So-in whimpered. Jin-wu walked into the hallway, pushing her aside. A gust of wind lashed Jin-wu across the back.

After that night, Jin-wu sometimes found himself awakened in the middle of the night by the sound of So-in's sobbing. Each time, he had a hard time suppressing his anger. He wished to kick and yell at her, "Go back to Korea!" But he didn't. At first, he thought that his visa problem was what held him

다음 날 오전에는 골드러시 체험 상품의 핵심 일정인 광산 탐방이 예정되어 있었다. 서인은 전등이 달린 안전모를 쓰고 허리를 굽힌 채 광산을 살펴보는 관광객들의 사진을 보여주었다.

　"금을 캐보는 거야?"

　진우의 질문에 서인은 피식 웃었다.

　"금이 계속 나오면 이런 탐방도 못 하지."

　서인의 말에 따르면 이미 150년 전에 문을 닫은 광산이었다. 그러니까 그들은 폐광을 둘러보러 가는 거였다.

　광산 체험 예약 시간보다 일찍 도착한 진우와 서인은 마을을 돌아다녔다. 마을이라고 해봐야 폐광 바로 옆에 붙어 있는 작은 박물관, 카페, 음식점 정도였다. 모두 문이 열려 있었지만 어디에도 손님은 보이지 않았다. 그 옆으로는 반쯤 무너진 집들이 즐비하게 서 있었다. 지붕이 모두 날아가 벽돌로 된 벽만 남은 모양이었다. 아주 오래전에 금광이었지만 이제는 아무것도 아닌 것을 중심으로 펼쳐진 마을은 몇 세기 전에 멸망한 왕조의 유적지처럼 보였다.

　서인이 카페에서 커피를 사는 동안 진우는 박물관을

back. However, even after he obtained the permanent residency, Jin-wu didn't tell So-in that it was okay now for her to go back to Korea. He thought she would leave him anyway without him having to tell her to. He even had a dream in which So-in was on her way out of their flat, carrying her suitcase and said, "It's alright now, isn't it?" But So-in didn't leave him. Instead, she suggested that they should take out a long-term home loan in his name. As she had done to find their own flat, So-in again did everything all by herself, busily visiting banks and real estate agencies, and finally found a detached house in the suburbs. The house, facing north, allowed plenty of sunlight in and had a spacious backyard. So-in planted colorful flowers as well as strawberry and tomato seedlings in the backyard. Quite often on holiday afternoons, Jin-wu would sit at the kitchen table and watch So-in working in the backyard with her back towards him. Wearing a wide-rimmed straw hat, she would skillfully turn over the soil, sow, pull out the weeds, and thin out the crowded leaves. Day by day, the backyard grew abundant. Eggplants and zucchinis were ripening and string beans and tomatoes were climbing along the support-bars that So-in had prepared for them. She often made salads with the vegetables from the backyard, which Jin-wu never even touched. As for

구경했다. 유리 전시장 안에 환한 빛을 발하는 커다란 돌이 있었다. 파도가 부서지는 바다처럼 푸른색과 흰색이 뒤섞여 있는 것으로 보였는데, 가까이 다가가자 오렌지색과 초록색이 반짝였다. 진우는 자리를 옮겨가며 그때마다 색이 변하는 돌을 한참 보았다.

"예쁘죠?"

가까이서 들리는 목소리에 진우는 흠칫 놀라 고개를 돌렸다. 양 볼이 붉은 여자가 진우의 바로 옆에 서 있었다. 여자는 자신의 손에 들려 있는 상자를 보여주었다. 상자에는 타원으로 세공된 보석이 박힌 반지가 여러 개 들어있었다. 모두 다른 색을 한 보석이 일제히 반짝였다.

여자는 보석에 대해 한참을 설명했는데 진우는 띄엄띄엄 옆 지역의 광산에서 나는 오팔이라는 정도만 알아들었다. 진우가 어색하게 끄덕거리자 여자가 푸른빛의 보석이 박힌 반지 하나를 상자에서 꺼내 내밀었다. 여자친구에게 주라는 것 같았다.

"아니요, 저는 결혼했어요."

진우는 손을 내저었다. 여자는 빙긋이 웃으면서 반지를 다시 내밀었다.

So-in, she ate up the salads without fail; she would rather that some of the soup or other side dishes got left over. Once in a while, she put a box of fresh vegetables in Jin-wu's car trunk, telling him to use them in the restaurant. Jin-wu always dropped by the park on his way to work and threw the box into the trash can there. In the end, So-in gave up on taking care of the backyard, letting nameless plants and weeds grow tall, some even up to his waist. Jin-wu looked at the abandoned jungle of a backyard and wondered which was worse: the yard full of vegetables that no one would eat or the yard overgrown with ugly weeds. The choice was beyond him.

The next morning, Jin-wu and So-in were scheduled to explore the mine, which was the highlight of the "Experience the Gold Rush" package. So-in showed Jin-wu a picture of a group of tourists. Wearing hard hats that had lamp attachments, the tourists were checking out the inside of a mine in a stooping posture.

"Are we gonna dig up some gold?"

At his question, So-in snickered.

"If gold were still discovered in this mine, we wouldn't be here having a tour like this."

According to So-in, the mine had stayed closed

"그럼 아내에게 주세요."

보석의 여기저기에서 밝은 빨강과 파랑이 나타났다가 사라졌다가 했다. 서인이 밖에서 진우를 불렀다.

광산 표지판이 붙어 있는 하얀색 철제구조물 위에 호주 국기가 나부끼고 있었다. 진우와 서인은 철제구조물 아래로 들어섰다. 그곳에는 바퀴 달린 손수레 하나가 놓인 좁은 철로가 깔려 있었다. 철로의 끝에 엘리베이터가 있었는데, 안전모를 쓴 키가 작고 통통한 금발의 여자가 그 앞에 서서 진우와 서인에게 손을 흔들어 보였다.

철근을 얼기설기 엮어서 만든 엘리베이터는 매우 작아서 사람 세 명이 타니 꽉 찼다. 진우와 서인, 그리고 자신을 가이드라고 소개한 여자는 몸을 붙이고 빠른 속도로 어둠 속으로 떨어졌다. 족히 1분이 넘게 지나고 엘리베이터 문이 열리자 뜨겁고 습한 공기가 덮쳐 왔다.

가이드가 엘리베이터 앞의 작은 공간에 모여 있던 열댓 명의 사람에게 안전모를 나눠주었다. 환한 빛이 나오는 전등이 달린 안전모를 쓴 진우와 서인은 무리를

for 150 years. That meant they were going to have a tour of an abandoned mine that morning.

Jin-wu and So-in arrived earlier than the scheduled time, so they set out on a tour of the village. It was doubtful if it could even be called a village. Right next to the mine entrance, there was a small museum, followed by a cafe and an eatery in a row, and that was about it. They were all open for business but not a single customer was seen in them. Nearby, a series of half-collapsed houses stood closely together. Their roofs had been blown away and only their brick walls still remained. The village, developed around the now completely insignificant cave despite its once-upon-a-long-time glory as a gold mine, looked like the site of a fallen dynasty that had been in ruins for centuries.

While So-in was buying coffee at the cafe, Jin-wu went into the museum. He was looking around inside when he saw a large stone brightly shining inside a glass display case. At first, it looked blue intermixed with white like the sea with its breaking waves; but when he stepped up to it, the stone began sparkling in orange and green. Jin-wu stared at the color-changing stone for a long time, walking around to see it from different angles.

"It's beautiful, isn't it?"

Hearing the voice right next to him, Jin-wu star-

따라 통나무를 이어 붙여 만든 통로를 걸었다. 통로의 끝에서 한 명씩 철근 사다리를 타고 내려갔고, 좁고 낮은 암석 터널에 다다랐다. 터널이 낮아서 진우는 허리를 다 펼 수가 없었다. 천장에는 굵은 철사 그물이 쳐 있어서 안전모가 철사에 긁히는 소리를 듣지 않기 위해 허리를 더 깊이 숙여야 했다.

철사 그물 아래에서 가이드는 일행을 향해 몸을 돌리고는 뒤로 걸으면서 설명을 시작했다.

"금광의 역사를 말해주고 있어."

서인이 속삭였다. 1800이라는 숫자가 반복해서 나오는 것을 보면 1800년대의 언젠가 금광이 시작되고 끝이 났으리라고 진우는 추측했다.

"겨우 18년이었대. 이 광산에서 금이 나온 게."

서인은 가이드의 말이 비는 공간을 찾아 진우에게 통역을 해주려 애썼는데, 여자가 끊임없이 말을 이어가 계속 멈춰야 했다.

"됐어."

진우는 이미 끝나버린 금광의 역사에는 아무 관심이 없었다. 서인은 설명을 안 들어도 괜찮겠냐고 몇 번 더 되묻고는 가이드 쪽으로 좀 더 가까이 다가섰다.

tled and turned his head to find a woman with rosy cheeks standing close to him. She showed him a box she was holding in her hand. Inside the box were several rings mounted with precious stones cut in the oval shape. The stones, all in different colors, were sparkling simultaneously.

The woman gave Jin-wu a long talk about the gems, but Jin-wu, catching a word here and another there, hardly understood her except that the gems were called opal and excavated in a mine in an area adjacent to the village. When Jin-wu nodded his head awkwardly, she took out a ring mounted with a blue stone from the box and held it out to him. She seemed to suggest that he should give it to his girlfriend.

"No, I'm married."

Jin-wu waved his hand. The woman smiled and held the ring out to him again.

"Give it to your wife, then."

Bright red and blue colors kept sparkling and fading here and there all over the stone. So-in called out to him from outside.

The Australian national flag was fluttering above the white-painted iron structure that had a mine signboard mounted on it. Jin-wu and So-in walked into the space underneath the iron structure. There

진우는 대열에서 조금 떨어져 벽을 만져보았다. 허옇게 살을 드러낸 암석을 타고 물이 흘러내렸다. 축축하고 울퉁불퉁한 벽이나 좁고 어두컴컴한 느낌이 어제 묵은 숙소와 비슷했다. 다만 서늘했던 숙소와는 달리 광산 내부는 숨이 막힐 정도로 뜨거웠다. 진우는 흐르는 땀을 훔치고 허리를 숙인 상태에서 고개를 들었다. 안전모에 달린 전등이 철사 그물 사이로 동그란 빛을 만들어냈다. 진우는 빛이 비치는 철사 그물 사이로 손을 집어넣었다. 그때 서인의 목소리가 날카롭게 울렸다.

"진우야!"

서인이 진우에게로 빠르게 걸어와 진우의 팔을 잡아챘다. 진우가 몸을 한껏 구부리고 있는 것과 달리 서인은 똑바로 서 있었고 어렵지 않게 진우의 팔을 끌어 내릴 수 있었다. 서인의 커다란 눈이 진우의 눈 바로 앞에 있었다.

"천장을 만지면 돌이 떨어질 수도 있어서 위험하대."

서인은 가이드가 천장을 만지면 안 된다고 몇 번이나 말했다고 했다. 그제야 진우는 사람들의 시선이 모두 자신을 향해 있는 것을 알아챘다. 진우는 사람들의

ran a narrow rail with a wheeled cart sitting idle on it. At the end of the rail was an elevator in front of which a short, plump, blonde woman in a hard hat stood, waving her hand to get Jin-wu and So-in's attention.

The elevator, built by weaving rebars crisscross, was very small; the three of them barely fit in it. Jin-wu, So-in, and the woman who introduced herself as their guide descended at a great speed into the dark, their bodies tightly packed in the narrow space. A full minute later, the elevator door opened, and Jin-wu and So-in were all at once overwhelmed by the hot and damp air flooding in.

The guide distributed hard hats to the group of about 15 people gathered in the small space in front of the elevator. Wearing the hard hats that cast bright beams of light from the mounted lamps, Jin-wu and So-in along with the rest of the group walked through a passageway built by connecting logs together. At the end of the passageway, they climbed down the rebar ladder one person at a time to arrive at a narrow and low rock tunnel. The tunnel was so low that Jin-wu had to stoop down since standing straight was impossible. Moreover, the ceiling was covered with thick-wire nets, so he had to bend his back further not to hear the noise made when the wire scraped his hard hat.

시선에 떠밀리듯 엉거주춤한 자세 그대로 벽에 기댔다. 발은 앞으로 내민 채 엉덩이를 벽에 붙이고 상체는 여전히 기울이고 있었다. 천장이 점점 낮아지는 것 같았고, 몸이 점점 더 접히는 것 같았다. 가이드가 진우를 바라보면서 큰소리로 뭔가 외쳤는데, 아주 짧은 문장이었는데도 제대로 알아듣지 못했다.

"앞으로."

서인이 진우를 잡아당겼다.

"벽에 기대지 말고 힘들면 차라리 앉으래."

서인이 진우의 어깨를 내리눌렀다. 진우는 털썩 주저앉았다. 축축한 바닥에 금세 바지가 젖었다. 서인이 가이드에게 사과하는 소리가 들렸다. 그가 영어를 잘하지 못한다고 했다. 진우는 고개를 들어 서인의 옆얼굴을 바라보았다. 서인은 자신이 광산을 뒤흔든 것처럼, 그래서 광산이 모두 무너져내린 것처럼 일그러진 얼굴을 하고 있었다.

점심을 먹고 출발한 탓에 운전하는 내내 오후 해가 차 안으로 깊숙이 들어왔다. 서쪽으로 달리고 있었다. 선글라스를 썼는데도 햇빛이 눈을 찔렀다. 해가 바로

Underneath the wire nets, the guide turned to-wards the group and started explaining while walk-ing backwards.

"She is talking about the history of this gold mine."

So-in whispered in Korean. Jin-wu heard the guide repeat the number 1800 and guessed that the gold mine had been opened and closed in the 1800s.

"It was only 18 years, she says. The period of gold excavation in this mine."

So-in tried hard to interpret for Jin-wu, using the time when the guide stopped talking before she started again. But the guide kept on talking without break, so So-in's interpretation was interrupted over and again.

"Don't bother."

Jin-wu was not interested at all in the history of the gold mine that had long been exhausted. After asking him a few more times if he was going to be all right without understanding the guide's talk, So-in moved closer to the guide.

Jin-wu moved a short distance away from the group, tempted to touch the wall. Water was flow-ing down over the exposed pale flesh of the rock. The damp and uneven wall as well as the sense of being enclosed in a narrow and dark space were

눈앞에서 타고 있는 듯했다. 앞에 있는 모든 것이 햇빛 안에서 부옇게 부서져버렸다. 서인은 잠들어 있었다. 해가 가득 내려앉은 서인의 얼굴을 보는데 쾅 하는 굉음과 함께 차창이 깨지며 차가 옆으로 휘었다.

브레이크를 밟고 정신을 차려보니 서인이 자신의 무릎을 내려다보고 있었다. 진우는 서인을 흔들어 괜찮냐고 물어본 후에 차에서 내렸다. 앞범퍼가 내려앉고 차체가 찌그러져 있었다. 진우는 다시 차에 타서 시동을 걸었다가 껐다.

"차는 괜찮아. 운이 좋았어."

"어떻게 된 거야?"

서인이 진우에게 물었다.

"캥거루를 쳤어."

"캥거루는 어떻게 됐어?"

"죽지는 않았어."

차는 차도에서 벗어나 끝없는 벌판을 향해 있다. 진우는 백미러로 캥거루가 몸을 일으키려고 애쓰는 것을 보고는 핸들에 이마를 댔다. 전날 길에서 마주친 캥거루를 떠올렸다. 그 캥거루는 지금 죽었을까. 아니면 아직도 뜨거운 해 아래서 딩고와 까마귀에게 살을 뜯

similar to what he had felt in the lodge the night before. Unlike the chill in the lodge, however, the air inside the mine was stiflingly hot. Jin-wu wiped off the sweat flowing down his face and raised his head while keeping his back still bent down. The lamp on his hard hat shot a cylindrical beam of light through the wire net. Jin-wu put his hand through the mesh lit by the lamp light. At that moment, So-in's sharp voice echoed in the tunnel.

"Jin-wu!"

So-in quickly walked up to Jin-wu and snatched his stretched arm. Unlike Jin-wu stooping as much as he possibly could, So-in was free to stand straight, which helped her bring his arm down easily. Now, So-in's big eyes were right in front of his.

"The guide says that touching the ceiling is dangerous because it may cause the rocks to fall."

So-in told him that the guide had warned multiple times not to touch the ceiling. Only then did Jin-wu realize all the eyes were turned on him. Jin-wu, as if to be shoved by their eyes, tipped himself backwards against the wall while remaining in the same half-standing posture. Now, his feet were on the ground a step away from the wall, but his behind was pressed against the wall while his upper body was still bent forwards. He felt as if the ceiling was coming down lower and lower and his body

어먹히며 죽음을 기다리고 있을까.

진우는 차에서 내려 트렁크를 뒤졌다.

"뭘 찾아?"

"캥거루를 죽이고 가야 할 것 같아."

진우는 타이어 레버를 찾았고 길을 건너 캥거루가 쓰러져 있는 초원으로 들어갔다. 가시풀에 다리가 쓸렸다. 캥거루의 뒷다리는 두 개 다 완전히 부러져 있었다. 부러진 곳에서 피가 흘러나와 낮은 풀을 적셨다. 캥거루는 앞다리로 몸을 절반쯤 일으킨 채 진우를 향해 으르렁거리는 소리를 냈다. 그러나 눈빛은 전혀 공격적이지 않았다.

"그냥 두고 가자."

서인이 소리쳤다.

"이미 죽은 거나 마찬가지야."

"어차피 죽을 거면 우리가 죽일 필요는 없잖아. 며칠이라도 더 살게 돼."

"여기 와서 봐. 피를 이렇게 흘리면 며칠도 못 버텨. 산 채로 물어뜯기게 될 거야."

진우는 심호흡을 한 뒤에 타이어 레버를 내리쳤다. 캥거루의 머리가 아래로 내리 찍혔다가 튀어 올랐다.

was being folded up tighter and tighter. The guide was looking at him, shouting something. It was a very short sentence, but he couldn't understand it.

"Forwards."

So-in pulled him towards her.

"Don't lean on the wall, she says. If it's too hard on your back, she'd rather you sat down."

So-in put her hands on his shoulders and pushed him downwards. Jin-wu slumped down on the ground. The wet ground immediately soaked his pants. He heard So-in apologize to the guide. She explained that he couldn't understand English well. Jin-wu raised his eyes and looked at the side of So-in's face. As if she was guilty of having shaken the whole of the mine down to the ground, her face looked distorted.

They left the lodge after lunch, so the afternoon sun came deep into the car the whole time he drove. He was driving west. Despite the sunglasses he had on, the sun smarted his eyes. It was as if the sun was blazing right before his eyes. All the landscape he saw ahead of him turned into exploding haze in the sunlight. So-in was asleep. He was looking at So-in's sunlight-soaked face when he heard a thundering noise and saw the windshield shatter; at the same time, the car was skidding.

한 번 더. 또 한 번 더. 빌어먹을. 또 한 번 더.

진우는 캥거루를 똑바로 내려다보지 못했다. 금방이라도 토할 것만 같았다. 차에 돌아와 피가 묻은 타이어 레버를 트렁크에 다시 넣고 나서야 티셔츠와 팔에도 피가 튄 것을 보았다. 진우는 티셔츠를 벗어 팔과 얼굴, 목을 닦았다. 얼굴과 목에서도 피가 묻어나왔다. 진우는 트렁크에 들어있던 가방을 열어 어제 입었던 티셔츠를 꺼내 입었다.

진우가 다시 운전석에 오르자 서인이 창밖으로 고개를 내민 채로 외쳤다.

"캥거루가 움직여."

진우는 사이드미러로 캥거루를 쏘아보았다. 캥거루는 움직이지 않았다.

"죽었어."

"분명히 움직였어."

진우는 차에 시동을 걸었다.

"캥거루가 살아 있다고."

서인의 목소리가 떨렸다.

"죽었어."

진우는 차를 출발시켰고 액셀러레이터를 밟았다.

He slammed on the brakes. Collecting himself, he saw So-in looking down at her own knees. Shaking her, Jin-wu asked if she was all right. He then got out of the car to find the front bumper collapsed and the body crushed. He got back in the car and started the engine and then turned it off.

"The car's alright. We're lucky."

"What on earth has happened?"

So-in asked Jin-wu.

"I've run over a kangaroo."

"What's happened to the kangaroo?"

"It's not dead, not yet at least."

The car had skidded off the road and was now facing the vast fields. When Jin-wu saw in the rear-view mirror the kangaroo struggling to raise itself, he pressed his forehead down on the steering wheel. The other kangaroo he had seen the previous day came to his mind. Is it dead yet? Or is it still waiting for its death under the hot sun while its flesh is being ripped open and devoured by dingoes and crows?

Jin-wu got off the car again, opened the trunk, and began rummaging it.

"What on earth are you looking for?"

"I think I'll have to kill the kangaroo before we move on."

Jin-wu found a tire lever. With the lever in his

한 시간이 넘도록 진우와 서인은 아무 말도 없이 길을 달렸다. 해가 지고 있었다. 여전히 서쪽을 향해서 달리고 있었으므로 그들 앞에 경이로운 노을이 펼쳐졌지만 둘 중 누구도 그에 관해 이야기하지 않았다.

진우가 불현듯 차를 멈추고 길옆에 세웠다.

"정말 캥거루가 움직였어?"

서인은 대답하지 않았다.

"정말 캥거루가 움직이는 걸 봤어?"

차 안으로 붉은 노을이 흘러들어왔다. 진우는 핸들을 움켜쥔 손등에 내려앉은 붉은 햇빛을 보다가 고개를 돌려 서인의 옆얼굴 역시 붉게 물들어 있는 것을 보았다. 진우는 주머니에 있는 오팔 반지를 생각했다. 진우는 서인에게 반지를 내밀며 무릎을 꿇은 적이 없었다. 사람들의 박수를 받으며 입장해 서인에게 입을 맞춘 적도 없었다. 초음파 사진을 보면서 눈물을 흘린 적도, 서인의 눈을 닮은 아이를 보며 경탄한 적도 없었다. 진우와 서인은 빛나는 순간을 가져본 적이 없었다. 빛나는 순간. 진우는 그것이 그들이 늘 기다려오던 것이라는 것을 알았다. 그리고 그것이 그들에게 절대 오지 않으리라는 것을 알았다. 붉은 햇빛이 차 안

hand, he walked across the road and into the scrubland towards the fallen kangaroo. Jin-wu's legs were scraped by burweeds. The kangaroo's hind legs, both of them, were broken completely. From the fracture wounds, blood poured out, drenching the short grass around them. Struggling to support its torso with the front legs, the kangaroo growled at Jin-wu. However, there was no aggressiveness at all in its eyes.

"Leave it and let's move on."

So-in yelled.

"It's as good as dead already."

"If it's gonna die anyway, we don't need to kill it now. Leave it be, let it live even for a few more days."

"Come here and see it for yourself. Bleeding at this rate, it's not going to last even a few days. It'll be eaten alive."

Jin-wu took a deep breath and swung the tire lever as hard as he could. The animal's head was smashed downwards and yet bounced right back. One more swing. And again. Damn it. And again.

Jin-wu dared not look straight down at the kangaroo. He felt sick. He came back to the car and tossed the blood-covered tire lever into the trunk. He then realized his T-shirt and even his arms were spattered with blood. He took off the T-shirt

에 가득 들어찼다. 진우는 온통 붉기만 한 세계를 바
라보았다.

and with it wiped his arms, face, and neck. Blood rubbed even off his face and neck. He opened his bag that was in the trunk, took out another T-shirt, the one he had on the previous day, and pulled it on.

When Jin-wu got back in the driver's seat, So-in shouted, poking her head out of the window.

"The kangaroo's moving."

Jin-wu stared at the kangaroo reflected in the side mirror. It didn't move.

"It's dead."

"No! It was most certainly moving."

Jin-wu started the car.

"It's alive, I'm telling you!"

So-in's voice trembled.

"It's dead."

Jin-wu pulled the car out and pressed down the accelerator pedal.

Longer than an hour, Jin-wu and So-in drove on, keeping silent. The sun was setting. They were still heading west, so a marvelous sight of the setting sun was unfolding before their eyes, but neither of them said anything about it.

In the end, it was Jin-wu who broke the silence. He suddenly pulled up the car by the roadside and said:

"Are you sure the kangaroo's still alive?"

So-in didn't answer.

"Did you really see it move?"

The red glow of the setting sun flooded the car. Jin-wu stared at the red sunlight that had settled on the backs of his hands that gripped the steering wheel; he then turned his head to find the side of So-in's face had been tinged with red as well. Jin-wu thought about the opal ring in his pocket. Jin-wu had never kneeled down before So-in, holding out a ring to her. He had never walked up the aisle and kissed So-in while being applauded by the well-wishers. Neither had he shed tears looking at an ultrasonic photo, nor uttered a cry of wonder at the sight of a baby that had So-in's eyes. Jin-wu and So-in had never had a shining moment together. A shining moment! Jin-wu knew that it was what they had always been waiting for. He also knew that the moment would never happen to them. The inside of the car was overflowing with the red sunlight. Jin-wu gazed out at the world that was glowing red everywhere.

창작노트
Writer's Note

2017년 J가 한국에 들어왔다. 이혼을 하기 위해서였다. J의 이혼에는 많은 문제가 얽혀 있었고, 조정과 소송이 이어졌다. 그 과정을 옆에서 바라보는 것이 몹시 고통스러웠다. 그러나 정작 J는 초연했다. 이혼을 결심하기 전이 더 괴로웠다고 했다. J는 자신이 겪고 있는 일을 누구에게도 알리지 않고 호주에서 오랜 시간을 혼자 보냈다. 그는 몇 주간 온종일 술을 마시고 30분 이상 잠을 자지 못했노라고 담담하게 말했다. 그때의 J와 함께 있어준다는 마음으로 이 소설을 썼다. 함께 술을 마시고 함께 욕을 하고 함께 울어준다는 마음으로

In 2017, J made a trip to Korea. The purpose of the trip was to get a divorce. The divorce was riddled with many problems that needed to be solved through a series of arbitration disputes and lawsuits. It was painful to watch the whole process from the side. J himself, however, maintained a detached attitude. He said the most agonizing time was before he made up his mind to go ahead with their divorce. Until he came to that decision, J had lived alone in Australia for a long time, without telling anyone about what he was going through. He had spent several weeks drinking night and day, unable to sleep more than a half hour a day, he

이 소설을 썼다.

소설을 쓰기 전에 J와 많은 이야기를 나눴다. 다 쓴 소설을 읽고 J는 마음이 아프다고 했다. 그 문자를 보고 나는 울었다. 소설 속 진우에게 빛나는 순간을 선물해주었다면 좋았을 것이다. 그가 서인을 떠나거나, 서인이 그를 떠날 수 있었을 것이다. 둘은 악수하면서 씩씩하게 헤어질 수 있었을 것이고, 사막이 아닌 다른 곳에서 빛나는 석양을 향해 미소지을 수 있었을 것이다. 그러나 진우와 서인은 그러지 않았다. 그것을 사랑이라고 부를 수 있을까.

나는 이 소설을 읽는 당신이 슬퍼하기를 바란다. 뒤뜰을 가꾸는 서인의 뒷모습을, 캥거루를 타이어 레버로 내리치는 진우의 뒷모습을 오랫동안 바라봐주기를 바란다. 지나가버린 사랑을 온 힘을 다해 움켜쥐고 있는 이들을 안쓰럽게 여겨주기를 바란다. 우리가 사랑을 포기하지 않음으로써 언젠가는 사랑에 다가갈 수도 있지 않겠냐고 말해주기를 바란다.

recounted later without losing his cool. I wrote this story as my way of going back in time and keeping J company in his darkest hours. In my mind, at least, I was drinking, cursing, and crying together with him in real time.

Before I started writing "Gold Rush," I had conversations with J on many occasions. When the story was completed, J read it and texted me that his heart ached. When I received the text message, I cried. It would have been better if I had given Jin-wu in the story a chance to experience a shining moment. If I had, one of the couple, either Jin-wu or So-in, might have been able to leave the other. They might have shaken hands, saying a high-spirited good-bye to each other; they could have beamed at the sight of glowing sunset in some place else than the desert. In the story, however, it never happens to Jin-wu and So-in. Can we call it—what they have left between them—love?

I hope you feel grieved while reading the story. Even after you finish reading, I hope, you will never stop gazing after So-in tending the backyard or Jin-wu striking the kangaroo down with the tire lever. I hope you can be sympathetic towards the couple who are clutching with all their might at their love

이 소설이 영문으로 번역된다는 소식을 듣고 나는 안젤라와 조지를 가장 먼저 생각했다. 그분들은 이 소설을 기쁘게 읽어주실 것이고, 집을 찾는 손님들이 모두볼 수 있도록 거실의 아름다운 장식장 위에 이 책을 올려놓으실 것이다. 내가 깊이 사랑하는 사람들에게 책을 선물할 수 있다는 것은 정말로 기쁜 일이다.

깊이 사랑하는 마음으로 계속 쓰겠다. 사랑을 쓰겠다. 손에 잡히지 않아도 포기하지 않고.

that is no more. I wish to hear you say: By not giving up on love, we may be able to come across it someday.

When I heard that this story would be translated into English, I immediately thought of Angela and George. I am certain that they will enjoy reading this story and then display the book on top of the beautiful cabinet in their living room so that all the visitors to their home can see it. I am so happy that I have books like this as my gifts to those towards whom I feel a profound love.

I will continue to write with deep love in my heart. I will try to give shape to love. I will never give up even if love keeps eluding my grasp.

해설
Commentary

쉬이 끝나지 않는, 미래 소망과
삶의 불확실성

선우은실(문학평론가)

미래란 무엇인가. 미래는 다가오는 시간성이다. 그러나 결코 도래하지 못하는 시간일지도 모른다. 현재에 대해 말하는 순간 현재가 이미 지나가버린 것이 되어 '지금' 존재하지 않는 것과 마찬가지로 미래 역시 포착되지 않는 시간성이기 때문이다. 미래가 정말로 '다가오는 것'이라면 그것은 늘 다가오는 상태로 존재한다. 어느 시점에서건 '다가오는 중'인 것을 무슨 수로 마주칠 수 있을까? 그렇다면 미래는 영영 오지 않을 시간이다.

이는 '미래'가 허구적이거나 무의미한 것임을 의미하지 않는다. 미래는 실물이 아니라 상태로 존재하는 것

Future Aspiration
and Uncertainty of Life Live On

Sunwoo Eunsil (Literary Critic)

What is the future? It is the time that is to come. At the same time, however, the future may be the time that is never to come. Once the present is mentioned, it is already part of the past that no longer exists 'here and now.' Likewise, the future is also an elusive concept of time beyond our grasp. If the future is really the time 'approaching' the present, it forever remains in the state of approaching. How can we encounter at any point of time what is always 'on its way' towards us? In this sense, the future is the time that will never arrive.

That, nevertheless, does not necessarily mean that the 'future' is fictitious or meaningless. It is just that because the future is not yet a concrete

이어서 감각의 차원에서 감지되는 것일 뿐이다. 미래를 감각하는 일은 실은 아주 흔하게 일어난다. 우리는 종종 현재를 담보 삼아 미래의 장면을 그린다. 그 과정에서 찬란한 미래를 위해 현실의 고충을 감내하며, 정반대로 바라는 미래가 그려지지 않기에 현재의 상태를 변화시키기도 한다. 우리는 '다가오는 것'으로서 미래를 현실로 마주하는 순간을 바라고 상상하면서 현재의 상황을 미래 가치로 환산한다.

그렇다면 고쳐 묻기로 하자. 미래는 어떻게 감각되는가? 미래는 언젠가 '현재'가 될 것이란 믿음과 희망에 기초해 관념적으로 구성된다. 중요한 것은 미래 이미지가 현실이 되든 그렇지 않든지의 여부와 관계없이 '다가올 것'으로서의 미래 그리기는 현실을 추동한다는 점이다. 희망하는 미래의 모습이 도래할지 그렇지 않을지 모르는 바로 그 상태가 미래를 구체적으로 감각하게 만든다. '머잖아 도래할 미래'라는 하나의 장면은 자신이 바라는 것으로서의 희망이지만 그것이 정말로 실현될지 어떨지는 알 수 없다. 원하는 시간이 오길 바라는 소망과 그 소망의 실현 (불)가능성을 점치는 일의 간극은 곧 불확정성으로 환원되며 불확실성과 불안

reality but in the state of approaching, we can only detect it within the realm of our senses. Sensing the future in fact occurs quite frequently; and when it occurs to us, we try to keep the picture of our envisioned future intact, often on the security of what is happening to us at present, that is, we try to find strength to endure present hardships for some splendid rewards in the future. In the same context, when our desired future seems unattainable, some of us try to change the present situations. Imagining and wishing to meet the 'approaching future-turned-present reality,' we convert the present situations into the future values.

Here, let's rephrase the opening question of this essay: How is the future sensed? The future gets ideologically constructed based on the belief and hope that someday it will become the 'present.' What is important is the fact that the act of envisioning the 'approaching' future, *whether it will be realized or not*, is what drives the present. The very state of uncertainty—not knowing if the desired future will come or not—allows us to have a concrete sense of the future. We may dream of a scene in 'the soon-to-be-fulfilled future,' but we never know if the dream will really come true. The discrepancy between hoping for the arrival of the

함을 발생시킨다. 그러한 미래 불확정성에 충분히 불안해했을 때, '미래'는 온다.

*

「골드러시」는 바라마지않은 미래가 현재로 도래해버린 시점의 이야기다. 소설에는 두 인물이 등장한다. 7년 전 호주 워킹홀리데이에서 만나 잠시 한국에 귀국해 혼인신고를 하고 호주로 돌아가 자리를 잡은 서인과 진우가 그들이다. 그들은 과연 과거에 무엇을 바랐는가?

서인은 한국에서의 정착을 원했으나 진우는 당시 일하던 식당의 주인으로부터 약속받은 "457 비자"를 포기할 수 없었기에 호주에서의 삶을 원했다. 진우는 "급여는 적어도 두 배, 경력을 고려하면 세 배가 될 터였고 법정 유급휴가 4주에 공공의료와 공교육이 무료"라는 말로 호주에서의 달라질 미래를 근거로 삼아 서인을 설득한다. 서인과의 행복한 미래란 보다 나은 벌이와 복지 혜택의 모습으로 구체화된다. 그러나 이러한 미래상은 그야말로 불확실한 것이다. 그런 미래가 찾

desired time and predicting the (un)attainability of that hope leads us back to indeterminacy, generating uncertainty and anxiety within us. It is when we become unsettled enough by the indeterminacy of the future that the future finally arrives.

*

The story "Gold Rush" tells about the time the two main characters' dearly desired future finally arrives. The main characters, So-in and Jin-wu meet for the first time seven years prior during their working holidays in Australia. After making a brief trip back to Korea to register their marriage, they settle down in Australia. What do they hope to accomplish in the future when they first meet?

So-in at first wants to settle down in Korea, but Jin-wu hopes for a life in Australia because he is unwilling to give up "the 457 visa" promised by the owner of the restaurant where he works at the time. Jin-wu wins So-in over by presenting to her their transformed future life in Australia: "the pay rise, doubled at the least or even tripled when his seniority was taken into account, four-week statutory paid vacation, and free public health care and public education." Jin-wu's idea of a happy

아오도록 만들기 위해서는 서인이 곁에 있어야 하고, 호주에서의 이민권을 문제없이 취득해야 한다. 진우는 그런 미래를 위해 현재의 몇 가지를 담보삼는다. 그중 하나는 일정 수준 이상 영어 시험을 통과해야 발급받을 수 있는 "457 비자"를 진우보다 영어를 잘하는 서인의 이름으로 발급받는 것이다. 서인이 이를 수락해 무사히 시험에 통과했고, 진우는 파트너 비자를 신청하면서 호주에서의 삶에 한 발짝 나아가는 듯 보인다.

찬란한 미래를 위한 또 하나의 담보는 진우의 업무 환경이다.

457 비자를 약속받기까지 진우는 최저시급의 70퍼센트만 받으며 일했다. 휴식 시간에도 쉬지 않았고 시프트로 받은 시간보다 매일 서너 시간씩 더 일했다. 사장은 진우의 휴무일에도 때때로 그를 불러서 종일 매장 재고 정리를 시키고 밥을 한 끼 사주고 들여보내고는 했다. 457 비자 신청 이후에는 최저시급으로 계산한 연봉보다 훨씬 웃도는 법정 금액을 지급해야 했기 때문에, 진우는 통장에 들어오는 급여의 절반을 사장에게 현금으로 되돌려주기로 약속했다. 사업체가 지급해야 하는 비

life together with So-in takes a concrete shape of higher incomes and better welfare benefits. However, the image of their future life is uncertain to say the least. To secure their dream future, Jin-wu needs So-in to be with him and to help obtain the immigrant status for both of them. So, Jin-wu puts up a few things in the present as a security for the future. One of them is to get "the 457 visa" issued in So-in's name since her English is more fluent than Jin-wu's, and therefore she has a better chance to pass the English proficiency test, one of the requirements to obtain the visa. So-in agrees with him, and as soon as she passes the English exam and gets the visa, Jin-wu applies for a partner visa, thus seemingly making a step forwards towards their life in Australia.

Another security for their splendid future is Jin-wu's work conditions.

Until he was promised the 457 visa application, Jin-wu had to settle for taking only 70 percent of the minimum wage. He never took breaks and everyday worked three or four hours longer than the number of hours assigned to his shift. Often, the owner asked Jin-wu to come into work even on his days off and had him take an inventory of the sales floor

자 신청비나 변호사비 따위도 모두 진우가 내기로 했다.

(18~20쪽)

진우가 행복한 호주에서의 미래를 성취하기 위해 당장 유지되어야 하는 조건은 현재 식당에서 "최저시급의 70퍼센트"를 받고 일하면서 기타 비자 관련 비용을 모두 진우가 부담하는 것이다. 즉 비자를 받기 위한 노동 착취에 '자발적'으로 가담하는 것이다. 앞서 진우는 서인에게 안정적인 업무 환경과 소득, 복지 혜택을 강조했지만 정작 그러한 권리를 얻는 미래에 가기 위해 바쳐져야 하는 것은 권리를 권리대로 누리지 못하는 종류의 노동이다. 이러한 아이러니함 속에서 진우가 바라는 미래는… 과연 올까?

*

서인을 설득해 비자를 따낸 지 얼마 되지 않은 시점, 서인은 자신의 외도를 진우에게 고백한다. 그녀는 진우를 더 이상 사랑하지 않는다며 한국으로 돌아가겠다고 우기고, 외도 사건이 유야무야 되는 동안 거처의 보

the whole day. The owner then treated Jin-wu to a meal before letting him go back to the share house. Once Jin-wu's application for the 457 visa was filed, the law obliged the restaurant owner to raise Jin-wu's annual salary to a much higher level than the pervious one which had been calculated at the rate of minimum wage. The situation forced Jin-wu to promise to return to the owner a half of the pay that would be deposited in his bank account, of course, in cash. Jin-wu also had to agree to take care of the visa application fee, the lawyer's fee, and so on, which the business owner was supposed to pay.

In order to fulfill his wish for a happy future in Australia, Jin-wu agrees to meet the unreasonable conditions forced upon him by the restaurant owner: accepting the pay rate at "the 70 percent of the minimum wage" and paying all the visa-related expenses out of his own pocket. In other words, to get the 457 visa, he "voluntarily" takes part in the exploitation of labor. While persuading So-in to settle down in Australia, Jin-wu emphasizes their rights, which will be guaranteed in the future, to safe work conditions, stable income, and welfare benefits. Nonetheless, he has to sacrifice those very rights in order to get to the future he dreams of. With his life

증금을 떼먹히기도 하는 등의 시련마저 끼어든다. 하지만 결과적으로 서인은 여전히 진우 곁을 지켜 그가 영주권을 취득한 이후의 삶에 함께 하고 있으며, 진우의 이름으로 장기대출을 받아 외곽에 주택을 구입해 비로소 안정적인 생활을 꾸린다. 그렇게 그들이 약속한 미래의 시간은 차근차근 현실로 도래했다. 문제는 미래의 '시간'은 도래했으나 그 미래의 '장면'이 아니라는 점이다.

진우는 언젠가 서인이 한국으로 돌아가겠다고 통보해올 것이라 여기며 하루하루 그들의 관계를 '연장'하는 마음으로 지내왔다. 그러나 서인은 헤어지자고 할 기미가 없고 결혼 7주년 맞아 '골드러시' 체험 행사에 가자고 말한다. 서인에 대한 조금의 애정조차 남지 않은 듯 보이는 진우는 마지못해 체험 행사에 끌려간다.

그들은 어째서 거의 끝난 것이나 다름없는 서로의 미래를 이토록 지난하게 이어가는가? 안정적인 관계를 바랐던 서인은 진우로부터 그것을 얻을 수 없었고, 영주권을 따고 정착하여 행복뿐인 미래를 그렸던 진우 역시 그러한 미래를 얻지 못했다. 그들의 미래 장면은 어그러진 채 그들의 현재로 다가왔고 그것은 빠르게

trapped in the irony of the situations, can Jin-wu indeed achieve his wished-for life in the future?

*

Not long after So-in, encouraged by Jin-wu, succeeds in obtaining the visa, Jin-wu learns of his wife's affair with another man. So-in says she does not love Jin-wu any more and insists on going back to Korea. While Jin-wu remains indecisive about what to do regarding his wife's adultery, they undergo some hardships including getting the security deposit on their rented room swindled. In the end, So-in ends up still staying with Jin-wu, even after Jin-wu gets his own permanent residentship. The couple even take out a long-term loan in Jin-wu's name, purchase a house in the suburbs, and finally settle down there. Their promised future has step by step become a reality. The problem is: their future 'time' has arrived, but it is not the future 'scene' they have envisioned.

Jin-wu continues to live with So-in, thinking that he is merely 'extending' their time together one day after another; at the same time, he believes that So-in will eventually say good-bye to him and return to Korea by herself. However, So-in shows no sign of

과거가 되어 돌이킬 수 없는 시간을 축적하고 있다. 이 시점에 그들이 예견할 수 있는 유일한 미래는 더 이상 서로가 함께 하지 않는 장면일지도 모른다. 그런데도 왜 서인은 뜻밖의 결혼 7주년을 기념코자 하며, 진우는 그 기념 행사에 속수무책 따라갔을까?

미래는 그것의 불확실성과 현재의 불안을 담보 삼아 구성된다고 말한 바 있다. 그러나 담보로 잡힌 그것들의 강도가 미래의 도래 가능성과 비례하는 것은 아니다. 힘든 일을 이만큼 감당했는데도 어떤 미래는 영영 오지 않는다. 도착하는 것이 '좀 뜻밖의 미래'일 때 유일하게 해야할 일은 그 뜻밖의 것을 완전하게 결말짓는 것뿐이라 여겨지기도 할 것이다. 이렇듯 어긋난 미래에 대한 완전한 종결 선고는 소설의 처음과 끝에 배치된 캥거루와 관련한 장면에 두드러진다. 첫 장면에서 죽어가는 캥거루는 이미 누군가에 의해 치인 상태였다. 캥거루의 직접적 죽음의 원인이 진우와 서인이 아니었기에 그들은 캥거루를 방치하고 지나가는 것을 선택할 수 있었다. 그러나 마지막 장면에서 캥거루를 친 것은 진우다. 진우는 결단을 내려야만 하는 상황에 놓여 다음과 같이 행동한다.

declaring their break-up; instead, she one day sug-gests they should take a trip together to join a tour program called 'Experience the Gold Rush' on the occasion of their seventh wedding anniversary. Jin-wu, who seems to have absolutely no love for So-in left in his heart, reluctantly agrees to go on the trip with her.

Why then do they continue to stay together, en-during excruciating pain all the while, when their relationship is as good as over? So-in is unable to enjoy the stable relationship she has dreamed of with Jin-wu; Jin-wu himself fails to realize his an-ticipated future, that is, a happy life after getting the permanent residentship and settling down in Australia. What they see now before their eyes is a distorted picture of their planned future; and, their present is quickly becoming their past, ac-cumulating time that will be forever lost to them. At this point of time, perhaps, the only future they may foresee is the one in which they no longer stay together. What then is the reasons for So-in's un-expected plan to celebrate their seventh wedding anniversary, or for Jin-wu's inability to refuse to go along with her plan?

As I stated above, the future is constructed on the security of the uncertainty of the future and the

차는 차도에서 벗어나 끝없는 벌판을 향해 있었다. 진우는 백미러로 캥거루가 몸을 일으키려고 애쓰는 것을 보고는 핸들에 이마를 댔다. 전날 길에서 마주친 캥거루를 떠올렸다. 그 캥거루는 지금 죽었을까. 아니면 아직도 뜨거운 해 아래서 딩고와 까마귀에게 살을 뜯어먹히며 죽음을 기다리고 있을까. (...)

"캥거루를 죽이고 가야 할 것 같아."

진우는 타이어 레버를 찾았고 길을 건너 캥거루가 쓰러져 있는 초원으로 들어갔다. 가시풀에 다리가 쓸렸다. 캥거루의 뒷다리는 두 개 다 완전히 부러져 있었다. 부러진 곳에서 피가 흘러나와 낮은 풀을 적셨다. 캥거루는 앞다리로 몸을 절반쯤 일으킨 채 진우를 향해 으르렁거리는 소리를 냈다. 그러나 눈빛은 전혀 공격적이지 않았다.

"그냥 두고 가자."

서인이 소리쳤다.

"이미 죽은 거나 마찬가지야."

(...)

진우는 심호흡을 한 뒤에 타이어 레버를 내리쳤다.

(58~60쪽)

anxiety of the present. Having said that, the value or volume of the security is not necessarily directly proportional to the likelihood of the planned future's arrival. Sometimes, it never comes even to those who have endured great ordeals. When a 'somewhat unexpected future' happens, we may think the only thing we can do is to bring the unexpected situation to a perfect closure. In the story, a perfect closure to a future that has gone amiss is vividly depicted at the beginning and the ending, in the scenes of injured kangaroos. In the first scene, there is a dying kangaroo that has already been run over by some other driver. Jin-wu and So-in choose to leave the kangaroo dying there, thinking that their choice is justified since they are not the direct cause of its death. However, in the ending scene, it is Jin-wu who runs over a kangaroo. He believes he is the one now who has to make a decision, and does as follows.

> The car had skidded off the road and was now facing the vast fields. When Jin-wu saw in the rearview mirror the kangaroo struggling to raise itself, he pressed his forehead down on the steering wheel. The other kangaroo he had seen the previous day came to his mind. Is it dead yet? Or is it still waiting

진우는 캥거루에게 완전한 선고를 내린다. 마치 서인과 진우의 이미 끝나버린 관계를 마침내 종언하듯이 '확실하게' 끝내고자 한다. 그렇게 하는 것이 겨우 연명하는 고통을 줄여줄 수 있으리라 생각했기 때문이다. 그러나 차를 출발시킨 뒤에 캥거루가 분명히 움직였다는 서인의 말을 그는 떨쳐버릴 수 없다. 캥거루가 정말 움직였냐고 재차 확인하는 진우가 마침 떠올리는 것은 골드러시의 체험 코스 중 하나인 폐광에서 한 여자가 팔던 반지다. 골드러시 행사 중 하나인 폐광 체험에서 "이미 끝나버린 금광의 역사에는 아무 관심이 없"었던 진우는 홀로 폐광을 돌아다니다가 반지를 파는 여자를 만난다. 여자친구가 없다면 아내에게 반지를 선물하라던 그 여자로부터 진우는 결국 반지를 구입했던 것이다.

　　차 안으로 붉은 노을이 흘러들어왔다. 진우는 핸들을 움켜쥔 손등에 내려앉은 붉은 햇빛을 보다가 고개를 돌려 서인의 옆얼굴 역시 붉게 물들어 있는 것을 보았다. 진우는 주머니에 있는 오팔 반지를 생각했다. 진우는 서

for its death under the hot sun while its flesh is being ripped up and devoured by dingoes and ravens? (...)

"I think I'll have to kill the kangaroo before we move on."

Jin-wu found a tire lever. With the lever in his hand, he walked across the road and into the grassland towards the fallen kangaroo. Jin-wu's legs were scraped by burweeds. The kangaroo's hind legs, both of them, were broken completely. From the fracture wounds, blood poured out, drenching the short grass around them. Struggling to support its torso with the front legs, the kangaroo growled at Jin-wu. However, there was no aggressiveness at all in its eyes.

"Leave it and let's move on."

So-in yelled.

"It's as good as dead already."

(...)

Jin-wu took a deep breath and swung the tire lever as hard as he could.

Jin-wu pronounces that the kangaroo must be put to death. As if to finally declare the end of his relationship with So-in, which has long been overdue, he decides to make an 'absolutely clear' ending. By doing so, he believes, he can minimize the

인에게 반지를 내밀며 무릎을 꿇은 적이 없었다. 사람들의 박수를 받으며 입장해 서인에게 입을 맞춘 적도 없었다. 초음파 사진을 보면서 눈물을 흘린 적도, 서인의 눈을 닮은 아이를 보며 경탄한 적도 없었다. 진우와 서인은 빛나는 순간을 가져본 적이 없었다. 빛나는 순간. 진우는 그것이 그들이 늘 기다려오던 것이라는 것을 알았다. 그리고 그것이 그들에게 절대 오지 않으리라는 것을 알았다. 붉은 햇빛이 차 안에 가득 들어찼다. 진우는 온통 붉기만 한 세계를 바라보았다. (64~66쪽)

분명 진우가 기다려왔던 "빛나는 순간"으로서의 미래는 오지 않았고 앞으로도 영영 오지 않을지도 모른다. 그것은 이미 되어버린 현재, 곧 되어버릴 과거다. 지금 진우가 마주한 '뜻밖의 미래'에서 그가 해야 하는 유일한 일은 '그려왔던 빛나는 미래'에 대한 확실한 종언처럼 보인다. 그러나 그들은 어째서 한때의 '드림'이었던 1800년대의 골드러시를 다시 체험하고 있으며, 진우는 끝내 그 반지를 사고야 말았던 것인가? 비록 회한에 젖을지라도 자신이 저당잡혔던 한 시절을 돌이켜보도록 만드는 시점에 이를 때, 그 '어긋남'의 시간들은

pain suffered while barely hanging on to life that is hopeless anyways. When he starts the car again, however, he cannot get out of his head what So-in has just said: she is certain that the kangaroo is still alive. Asking her for the second time if she has really seen the kangaroo move, he is suddenly reminded of the ring he has bought from a sales woman in the museum just before exploring the abandoned mine that is the highlight of the "Experience the Gold Rush" travel package. As a matter of fact, Jin-wu is "not interested at all in the history of the gold mine that had long been exhausted," but when he meets the sales woman inside the museum, he ends up buying the ring from her who tells him to give the ring to his girlfriend or his wife if he is already married.

The red glow of the setting sun flooded the car. Jin-wu stared at the red sunlight that had settled on the backs of his hands that gripped the steering wheel; he then turned his head to find the side of So-in's face had been tinged with red as well. Jin-wu thought about the opal ring in his pocket. Jin-wu had never kneeled down before So-in, holding out a ring to her. He had never walked up the aisle and kissed So-in while being applauded by the well-wishers. Neither

단단하게 응축되어 '지금'을 강력하게 환기시킨다. 소설의 제목 '골드러시' 그 자체와 같이, 골드러시 체험 중 진우가 사고 말았던 '오팔 반지'처럼 말이다.

*

하나의 시간이 끝났음을 선고하는 일은 단순히 미래의 실패를 의미하지 않는다. 어떤 것이 흘러간 시간이 되어버렸을 때 그것은 추체험되기 시작한다. 이 서늘한 종언의 서사는 '지나가 버린 미래'일지라도 그것에 대한 동경이 쉬이 끝나지 않을 것임을 암시한다. 그리고 바로 지금, '더 이상 미래 없음'의 시점에서도 그 이후에 대한 어렴풋한 기대가 지금 어떤 관계를 완전히 끝장내지 못함을, 미래로 향하는 삶의 불확실성이란 그런 식으로 삶을 지속시킨다는 것을 우리는 조금씩 알아간다.

had he shed tears looking at an ultrasonic photo, nor uttered a cry of wonder at the sight of a baby that had So-in's eyes. Jin-wu and So-in had never had a shining moment together. A shining moment! Jin-wu knew that it was what they had always been waiting for. He also knew that the moment would never happen to them. The inside of the car was overflowing with the red sunlight. Jin-wu gazed out at the world that was glowing red everywhere.

Obviously, the "shining moment" of the future anticipated by Jin-wu has not come and it may never come. The failed dream is now his present and will soon become his past. Faced with the 'unexpected, distorted future,' he seems compelled to finally pass a death sentence upon the 'splendid future he has pictured.' But then, he and So-in join the tour program that re-enacts the historical Gold Rush that once was 'the collective dream' of the 1800s. Why? Furthermore, what makes Jin-wu end up buying the ring? There is no doubt that he is overwhelmed with bitter remorse. However, when he is reminded of those days of his life put on hold as a security for the future, the 'ironies and distortions' of the past become condensed solid, calling attention to the 'present' with an irresistible power, as powerful as the attraction of the "Gold Rush," as solid as the 'opal ring' Jin-wu buys while on the Gold Rush tour.

*

Pronouncing the end of a time does not simply mean the failure to have the anticipated future arrive. Once something passes into the bygone times, it then begins to be re-experienced in one way or another. The terrible pronouncement of death paradoxically alludes to the fact that the aspiration for the future is hard to die even after it becomes the 'bygone future.' And now, at this moment of 'no more future,' some expectation for the 'thereafter,' faint as it may be, holds one back from ending the present relationship once and for all. Thus, we learn little by little that is the way the uncertainty of the future has us carry on with our lives.

비평의 목소리
Critical Acclaim

소설은 광산에서의 여행 일정을 소화하는 진우와 서인의 현재와 과거의 연애와 결혼생활을 병치시키며 관계의 틈이 벌어져온 과정을 보여준다. 워킹 홀리데이로 간 호주에서 처음 만난 두 사람은 삼 개월 만에 결혼했다. 결혼한 지 일 년이 지나 진우는 서인이 다른 남자와 잤다는 사실을 알게 되지만, "영주권을 받을 때까지만" 관계를 유지하자며 그녀를 붙잡았다. 그렇게 "어느 편이 더 나은지 알 수 없"는 상태로 칠 년이 지났다. 이런 두 사람이 "빛나는 순간"을 가져볼 수 있을까. 컴컴한 광산 안에서 "동그란 빛" 하나도 손에 쥐지 못하는데, 손을 뻗은 순간에 위험을 알리는 짧은 문장도 알아듣지 못하는데, 과연 그것이 가능할까. 이 물음에 응답하듯 여행에서 돌아가는 길에 또다시 만난 캥거루를 진우는 차로 받고, 심지어 "캥거루를 죽이고 가야 할 것 같"다며 타이어 레버로 내리쳐 부러 죽인다. 마치 겨우 숨이 붙어 있는 관계를 제 손으로 끝맺음하겠다는 듯. "빛나는 순간" 같은 건 "그들에게 절대 오지 않으리라는 것"을 되새기는 듯. 캥거루가 움직였다고 말하는 서인에게 죽었다고 거듭 말하는 것도 그러한 이유에서일 것이다. 결코 오지 않을 미래를 떠올리는 두

Although "Gold Rush" begins with a couple, Jin-wu and So-in, starting on a trip to a gold mine, the story in fact has another plotline that develops parallel to the first one. The second plotline reveals the couple's past, that is, how they meet, fall in love, get married, and eventually become estranged from each other. Jin-wu and So-in meet for the first time in Australia during their respective working holidays; and three months later, they get married. At the end of the first year of their marriage, Jin-wu comes to learn that So-in has been sleeping with another man. Nevertheless, Jin-wu pleads with So-in to stay married to him "only until he gets his permanent residentship." In that noncommittal, not knowing "which was worse" state of affairs, they stay together for seven more years. Is it possible for these two to experience a "shining moment" of life together? When nothing seems to be within their grasp, not even the small "circle of light" inside the dark mine or the short sentence warning about the danger of touching the cave ceiling, will they ever be able to get a chance to enjoy a "shining moment"? As if to answer this question, Jin-wu, when he happens to run over a kangaroo on the way back home from the trip, pronounces he has "to kill the kangaroo before ... move on," and strikes the animal down with a tire lever. As if determined to put an end to their relationship that barely hangs

사람의 시야가 붉게 물든다. 호주의 붉은 노을에 방금 전 죽음을 맞은 한 생명의 피가 겹쳐지는 순간, 행복을 꿈꾸었던 나라에서 파국을 향해 가는 두 사람의 관계 또한 읽는 이에게 생생한 이미지로 와닿는다.

소설의 끝에서 제목에 담긴 의미를 다시 한번 헤아려본다. '골드러시'는 결혼 칠 주년을 맞아 떠난 여행의 체험상품이기도 하지만, 호주에서 영주권자로 살기를 택한 진우와 서인의 삶을 뜻하는 것이기도 하다. 이주노동자의 삶을 적극적으로 점에서 생각할 거리를 남기는 작품이다.

소유정, 「가질 수 없는 빛」, 『문학동네』 2021년 봄호.

서수진의 『코리안 티처』는 구체성과 실감이 좋은 이야기를 만드는 데 얼마나 크게 기여하는지 여실히 보여주는 소설이다. 작가는 외국인 대상의 한국어학원 운영 실태를 핍진하게 묘사함으로써 어학원이라는 실용적 공간을 우리 사회가 처한 여러 현안이 혼용된 문제적 공간으로 확장한다. 화자로 제시된 네 명의 여성 강사는 소비재처럼 단기가 사용되고 평가되고 쉽게 교

onto life, as if reminding himself that such thing as a shining moment will never happen to them, he repeatedly enunciates that the kangaroo is dead to So-in who insists that it is still alive and moving. The couple who expect no bright future coming their way see everything in their fields of vision drenched red. As the red glow of the Australian sunset overlaps with the blood of a being that has just met its death, the vivid image of the two people heading for the end of their marriage, in a country where they once dreamed of a happy life together, comes home to the reader.

After reading the story, I cannot help pondering on the meaning of the title once more. "Gold Rush" is not only the name of the tour program the couple join on the occasion of their seventh wedding anniversary, but also signifies the life of Jin-wu and So-in who choose to settle down in Australia as permanent residents. As a probing study of the lives of emigrant workers, the story gives the reader food for thought.

So Yu-jeong(Critic)

Seo Su-jin's *Korean Teacher* plainly shows how much contribution concreteness and realness make to the creation of good works of fiction. By authentically depicting in this novel the realities of

체되는데, 이를 통해 여성이 학력, 직업, 계급, 국적과 상관없이 얼마나 쉽게 약자로 전락하는지를 가독성 갖춘 반듯한 문장으로 보여준다. 젠더 문제뿐 아니라 유학생 간의 인종차별 문제, 외국인노동자의 현실, 유학생 국적을 둘러싼 글로벌 계급 문제를 되짚어봄으로써, 우리가 그간 지향하던 글로벌이나 세계화라는 것이 얼마나 허약하고 위악적인 표어였는지를 새삼 깨닫게 된다.

실제를 그대로 전달한다고 소설이 되는 것은 아니지만 실제처럼 여겨져야 이야기의 진실이 전해지는 좋은 소설이 된다는 것을 이 작품을 통해 확인할 수 있었다.

편혜영, 제25회 한겨레문학상 수상작 『코리안 티처』(2020) 추천의 말.

managing an academy that teaches the Korean language to foreigners, the writer turns the practical space of the academy into a microcosm of our society where a variety of pending problems interact. The four female Korean teachers are the narrative voices of the novel. Like consumer goods, they are appraised and used for a brief period of time before being nonchalantly replaced by the hands of the management. The writer uses a decent and easy-to-understand narrative style to demonstrate how easily women, regardless of their educational backgrounds, types of work, ranks, or nationalities, are turned into social underdogs. By retracing such issues as gender, racism among foreign students, the realities of foreign workers, and the global class system in relation to the nationalities of foreign students, the writer has us realize afresh how we all have been misled by the slogan "globalization," which is in fact nothing but a fragile and pernicious catch phrase.

Simply describing realities as they are may not necessarily constitute a work of fiction. Having said that, the sincerity of the story, which I believe is the very essence of good fiction, gets conveyed only when it reads like a faithful portrayal of reality as in *Korean Teacher*.

Pyun Hye-young(Writer)

K-픽션 030
골드러시

2021년 6월 30일 초판 1쇄 발행

지은이 서수진 | 옮긴이 전미세리 | 펴낸이 김재범
기획위원 전성태, 정은경, 이경재, 강영숙
인쇄·제책 굿에그커뮤니케이션 | 종이 한솔PNS
펴낸곳 (주)아시아 | 출판등록 2006년 1월 27일 제406-2006-000004호
주소 경기도 파주시 회동길 445
전화 031.955.7958 | 팩스 031.955.7956 | 홈페이지 www.bookasia.org
ISBN 979-11-5662-173-7(세트) | 979-11-5662-550-6 (04810)
값은 뒤표지에 있습니다.

K-Fiction 030
Gold Rush

Written by Seo Su-jin | Translated by Jeon Miseli
Published by ASIA Publishers | 445, Hoedong-gil, Paju-si, Gyeonggi-do, Korea
Homepage Address www.bookasia.org | Tel.(8231).955.7958 | Fax.(8231).955.7956
First published in Korea by ASIA Publishers 2021
ISBN 979-11-5662-173-7(set) | 979-11-5662-550-6 (04810)

바이링궐 에디션 한국 대표 소설 목록